69 THINGS TO DO WITH A DEAD PRINCESS

Stewart Home was born in South London in 1962. When he was 16 he held down a factory job for a few months, an experience that led him to vow he'd never work again. After dabbling in rock journalism and music, Home switched his attention to the art world in the 1980s and now writes novels as well as cultural commentary.

69 THINGS TO DO WITH A DEAD PRINCESS

Stewart Home

CANONGATE

First published in Great Britain in 2002 by
Canongate Books Ltd, 14 High Street,
Edinburgh EH1 1TE

10 9 8 7 6 5 4 3 2 1

British Library Cataloguing-in-Publication Data
A catalogue record for this book is available on
request from the British Library

ISBN 1 84195 182 X

Typeset by Palimpsest Book Production Limited,
Polmont, Stirlingshire
Printed and bound by
Creative Print and Design, Ebbw Vale, Wales

Hobbity-style map drawn by Charly Murray

www.canongate.net

'I regard truth as a divine ventriloquist. I care not from whose mouth the sounds are supposed to proceed, if only the words are audible and intelligible.'
Coleridge, *Biographia Literaria*.

'I am a machine condemned to devour books.'
Marx in a letter to his daughter Laura dated 11 April 1868.

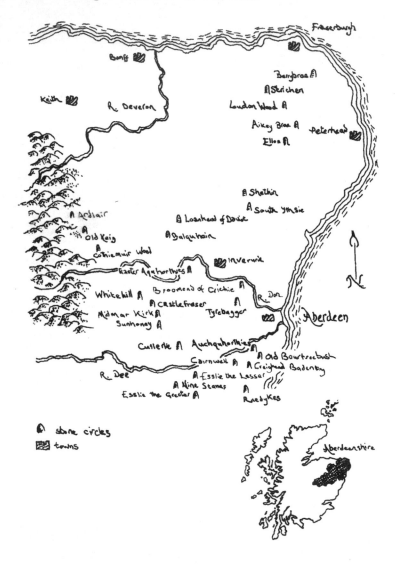

Selected Aberdeenshire Stone Circle Sites

Fraserburgh

Banff

Bennybrea
Strichen
Keith
R. Deveron
Loudon Wood
Aikey Brae
Peterhead
Ellon

Shethin
South Ythsie

Ardlair
Loanhead of Daviot
Old Keig
Balquhain
Cothiemuir Wood
Inverurie
Easter Aquhorthies
Broomend of Crichie
R. Don
Whitehill
Castle Fraser
Tyrebagger
Aberdeen
Midmar Kirk
Sunhoney

Cutlerie
Auchquhorthies
Cairnwell
Old Bourtreebush
R. Dee
Craighead Badenby
Esslie the Lesser
Nine Stanes
Esslie the Greater
Raedykes

stone circles
towns

Aberdeenshire

ONE

A MAN who no longer called himself Callum came to Aberdeen intent on ending his life. He wanted to die but not by his own hand. That was where I came in. He wanted me to help him act out his death. A psychodrama. When I met Callum he told me his name was Alan.

It was a cold overcast day. I'd slept late and abandoned my plan to go to the beach. I liked going to the beach. Even in winter. Even at night. But not when it was wet. I went to Union Street. I didn't have anything better to do. The shops were filled with commodities but they bored me. Books. Records. The Aberdeen merchants didn't cater for tastes like mine. I relied on secondhand stores, mail order, presents from friends, trips to Edinburgh and London. Things could have been worse. I could have been living in Dundee where the rents were cheaper but the city centre was a pedestrianised shopping nightmare. Aberdeen was better, there was the beach, Union Street and oil money. If Brighton was San Francisco on the South Coast, then Aberdeen was Los Angeles on the North Sea.

It was a dreary mid-week lunchtime and the pubs were unusually empty. I took advantage of this to avoid my friends. I went to The Grill, a very traditional bar. I'd not been to The Grill before despite the place being legendary. The old men who patronised The Grill were reputed to dislike women drinkers. I'd heard the management were

1

endlessly deferring the installation of a ladies' toilet. This ensured the regulars enjoyed a predominantly male environment.

I walked in to a dozen hostile stares. Alan looked up from a book, waved at me and said afternoon. I misheard what he said, it wasn't quite 12.30 and I thought Alan was saying my name. Anna Noon. I didn't recognise Alan but I thought he must know me. I went and sat with him. He got up and bought me a drink. I looked at the book he was reading. *However Introduced to the Soles*, new poetry from Niall Quinn, Nick Macias and Nic Laight. Alan returned with my gin and a fresh pint of heavy. I asked him to read me his favourite poem in *However Introduced to the Soles* and he recited the contents page from memory.

I added tonic to the gin and raised the glass to my lips. Old men were swimming before my eyes. A struggle to keep up with the times was written across their blank faces. The town had changed. Oil had changed the town. The old men drank slowly, preserving as best they could their pensions and their memories. Things were different in the old days. Oil had turned their world upside down. House prices had gone through the roof. Their children had moved away. They couldn't afford to live in the city. Aberdeen had changed. I didn't want to speak. I didn't want Alan to speak. We both had English accents. Neither of us was involved with the rigs.[1]

I finished my drink and suggested we relocate to one of the pubs near the station. My shout. Alan said we could go back to his place. I didn't know if this was a suggestion or a threat. He had a bottle of Springbank. I didn't know what it was. A Campbeltown malt, he explained. Alan also had a bottle of gin. That was good enough for me. It was raining. Neither of us had an umbrella. Alan paid for a taxi to Union Grove. It wasn't far. East of the big detached houses favoured by the oil men. The door to the tenement needed a new coat of paint. The stairs needed sweeping. Alan's flat was on the first floor.

We went through the door. I'd never seen anything like it. There were books everywhere. Bookcases, even in the hallway, covered every inch of wall space, from the floor to the ceiling. But there wasn't enough shelf space for the books. There were piles of books lying all over the floor. Old newspapers too. Alan led me into the living room. It was filled with books. I was surprised by the furniture, carpets and curtains. Brown leather and chrome. Brown shag pile. Blue velvet. Someone had spent money on the flat. Although the colour combinations left a lot to be desired, I was envious. Take away the books and the flat would have been fabulous. It was much better than my bedsit.

I gestured at the books, piled high on shelves, on a table, on the floor. What is this? Alan told me it was an occult memory system. Then he left the room. There were letters at my feet. Bills. They were addressed to Callum MacDonald, Flat 3, 541 Holloway Road, London. Alan came back with whisky and gin, ice and a lemon. Alan was organised, even if his flat was a mess. What was he wearing? If I'd known I was going to write about him later, I'd have made some notes at the time. He didn't like to stand out in a crowd. Alan often wore black Levi's, lace-up shoes, an open shirt and a dark jacket. Since it was cold, he'd have been wearing a V-neck jumper. He had several raincoats, all dark. He'd have taken off his coat and jumper once we were inside the flat. The central heating was on and double glazing kept the rooms warm.

I took a sip of gin and asked Alan what he did. He told me he read and that when he'd finished reading, he'd die. I asked him why he'd come to Aberdeen. He told me he'd inherited the flat and the books it contained. When I asked if his parents were rich he laughed. The flat hadn't belonged to his family, it had been owned by an older woman who'd become very fond of him. Alan kicked over a pile of books and told me he'd only been in Aberdeen a few days. He wanted to clear the flat, the books irritated him. I suggested that Alan try the Old Aberdeen Bookshop, an emporium close to the university that specialised in quality secondhand stock. Alan laughed. He was going to read every one of the books before he got rid of them.

Alan picked up the paperbacks he'd kicked over. A selection of titles by Erich Fromm. He told me the books were rubbish. He hurriedly read aloud from the introductions to *The Art of Loving*, *The Revolution of Hope*, *To Have or to Be* and *The Anatomy of Human Destructiveness*. In each introduction Fromm repeated himself, apologising for the repetition of material between his new book and his previous texts but justifying it on the grounds that it provided the necessary framework from which the reader could understand the fresh insights his latest work contained. Alan asked me if I was familiar with Fromm's work. No. He gave me *Escape from Freedom* and told me to keep it. He had an English edition of the book put out by RKP. The title was *Fear of Freedom* but the text was identical to the American edition with the original title. I have both books now. Soon after we met, Alan started selling the books he'd read to the Old Aberdeen Bookshop. I'd go over to the shop once or twice a week, picking up whatever Alan off-loaded.

I asked Alan how old he was. He claimed to be 36. At first I thought he was joking. I thought he might be two or three years older than me. We got along easily enough, maybe it was the gin. It didn't feel like there was a 16-year age gap between us. I asked Alan if he wanted to have sex. He led me through to the bedroom and asked me if I'd mind being tied up. I was reluctant until he promised not to hurt me. Alan tied my hands behind my back. He put a blindfold over my eyes, then placed a hood over my head. He rolled me onto my stomach and touched my spine and the tops of my legs. He touched the back of my knees. Put my toes in his mouth and sucked them. He crawled all over me. Moved my limbs around and licked under my armpits. By the time he got me to shift my arse and shoved two fingers into my cunt, I was dripping wet.

I suspect Alan wasn't using a condom when he fucked me. If he was it burst, because afterwards I could feel his come dripping out of my cunt. Alan threw a blanket over me and then he left. I don't know how long I lay there. Alan had told me not to move and that he would be back. I was aroused. I drifted in and out of sleep. Erotic dreams. Erotic thoughts. I trusted Alan. I liked the sensation of his come dripping out of my cunt. I liked feeling helpless and I was overcome with excitement when I heard Alan's voice again after what seemed an infinity of sleepless dreams and dreamless sleep.

I thought it was Alan fingering my cunt. Climbing on top of me. Ramming his big stiff cock up my creamy hole. I thought it was Alan because all the while I could hear his voice. He told me that I was the best-looking girl in the world. That I really turned him on. That he wanted to get me pregnant. Alan fell silent but I could feel hot breath on the back of my neck. Then something strange happened. There were two hands beneath me, fondling my breasts. A different pair of hands removed my hood and stroked my hair. This second set of hands lifted my head up, fingers found their way into my mouth. Then the fingers were joined by a cock. I was still being fucked doggie-style from behind. The fingers wet with my saliva were playing with my hair. I didn't know who, couldn't see who, I was giving a blow job.

Fingers fumbled with the blindfold, removed it. I looked up and saw Alan. Now I knew who I was sucking but I didn't know who was fucking me. With the corner of my eye I could see a ventriloquist's dummy. I'd noticed it earlier, when I first entered the bedroom, before I'd been tied up and blindfolded.[2] I was coming, I could taste Alan's spunk in my mouth, I felt the other man's prick harden and then he shot his load. Alan withdrew his cock from between my lips and put the hood back over my head. I could hear someone dressing, they left. Alan was undoing the rope that bound my wrists. We curled up together, under the blankets, fell asleep.

We didn't doze for long. Alan woke me getting out of bed. I watched him dress. A book-lined wall behind him. When he started pulling books from shelves I hauled myself out of bed. Alan told me that you had to treat books well, move them around, show an interest, or they'd die just like plants. He complained that he'd expected to find something more than commercially published paperbacks. His friend had been a magus and although there were occult titles, these were vastly outnumbered by philosophy, politics, literature, history, sociology and plenty of other topics. We went through to the sitting room and had another drink. I picked up the Erich Fromm book that Alan had given me. My host said Fromm criticises mechanisation precisely because his literary technique is mechanised. At that moment I wasn't certain I understood what Alan meant, but as I acquired more of his books I realised there was nothing much to understand.

Alan criticised Fromm for denouncing a mechanical culture of death so that it might be endlessly reproduced under the rubric of life. Alan compared Fromm's conception of a social character to Spengler's agrarian mysticism and the claim that there are distinct social types to be found in

the countryside and the city. When I said I didn't know
what he was talking about, Alan suggested I take his copy
of *Decline of the West* if I wished to waste a few hours with
right-wing froth. Alan picked up Fromm's *The Anatomy of
Human Destructiveness*. I have his 1977 Penguin paperback
edition in front of me as I write. He opened the book at
page 440 and pointed to what Fromm had to say about the
slogan 'Long live death!' Alan found a copy of Alexander
Herzen's *From the Other Shore* and pointed out that the
Russian populist used the slogan 'Vive la mort! And may
the future triumph!' at the end of a letter written in Paris
on 27 July 1848.[3]

Alan criticised Fromm for understanding neither the
historical genesis of the slogan 'Long live death!' nor its
meaning. He pulled a copy of Victor Hugo's *Les Misérables*
from a shelf and showed me a passage where the crowds
manning the Parisian barricades of 1832 are depicted shout-
ing 'Long live death!' He made me look at Marx's two
texts about 1848, *The Class Struggles in France* and *The
Eighteenth Brumaire*. He stressed that the latter work begins
with the famous observation that history repeats itself, the
first time as farce, the second as tragedy, and according
to Alan this is exactly what happened in Spain during
the civil war. Then he picked up Francis Fukuyama's *The
End of History and the Last Man* and drew my attention
to a quote at the beginning of chapter 13 from Hegel's
Phenomenology concerning the master/slave dialectic. Alan
muttered that even a right-wing cretin like Fukuyama had
advanced further in his superficial reading of Hegel than
Fromm.

Alan kicked several Fromm books across the room. Dismissing them and their author for ignoring the death of
Socrates as an act of scapegoating that gave birth to Western
philosophy. Alan insisted that any philosopher or occultist

worth their salt could tell you that death is the supplement of life, just as life is the supplement of death, that we only start living in death. The ability to imagine our own death not only makes us human, it may yet make us divine. Fromm imagined he was a Marxist and yet he completely ignored what Hegel had to say about death. After observing that even Norman O. Brown was preferable to Fromm, Alan picked up his coat and suggested we went out and got something to eat.

We went to La Bonne Baguette and ate French onion soup with bread. Alan drank espresso, I drank cappuccino. I asked Alan how many people he knew in Aberdeen. He said he didn't know anyone, I was the first person he'd befriended, he'd only been in the city a couple of days. If Alan didn't know anyone, I wanted to know who he'd got to fuck me. He said Dudley had fucked me. Dudley who? Dudley Standing. Who was Dudley Standing? The ventriloquist's dummy I'd seen in the bedroom, Alan had brought it up from London. I told Alan not to be ridiculous. Alan asked if I'd believe he'd just gone and grabbed some 20-year-old boy off the street. I found this idea very sexy. I could feel my knickers getting wet.

After our soup we went to the Prince Of Wales. We met some guys I knew there. Alan wanted to leave after one drink. Gareth told me he'd spent the day writing an essay. Alan said that both sperm and ink flowed out. From semen to semantics, he was alluding to what we'd being doing since lunchtime. We tried the Blue Lamp. Suzy and Jill waved us across to their table. Suzy had just split up with her boyfriend, Jill was trying to comfort her. We sat with them for a while. Alan asked me if I'd ever gone down on another woman. I said no. He asked me if I'd read *69 Things to Do with a Dead Princess* by K. L. Callan. Again my answer was negative.

After a while Suzy and Jill were drawn into our conversation. Chitchat mainly about films and books but somehow the talk became serious. Jill said that Lynne Tillman was the best living writer she'd read. Alan observed that 'best' wasn't an appropriate term to apply to literature. Then he began talking about Angus Wilson's endless and unintentional deconstruction of literary form. According to Alan, by reproducing an apparently banal set of values Wilson was able to illustrate what he was unable to declare – that there were no foundations to knowledge. The gap between what Wilson set out to do, and what he actually did, exposed literary discourse for what it was – a fable without beginning or end that presupposed its own origins in a mythological superiority to other textual forms. Angus Wilson and William McGonagal were the only two writers Alan would recommend without hesitation to anyone who solicited his opinion about what they should read.

I went to the toilet with Jill. She'd overheard Alan telling me earlier that he'd like to get off with her. Jill dared me to undo Alan's flies and take his cock out, so that she could see it. It seemed like a good idea at the time. We sat back down at the table. Alan was snogging Suzy. He had his hand inside her knickers. I put my hands on his crotch, undid the button fly on his jeans, took his prick out. It was soft and squidgy but quickly hardened in my hand. Jill stroked Alan's erect tool and it sprang up out of my palm. We giggled, then put the phallus away, I was worried someone outside our little circle might notice I'd taken it out. Jill suggested we go back to her place. We all agreed so Alan bought some carry-out beers and we split.

Jill shared a flat with a girl called Karen. Jill's flatmate was asleep. We were drunk, still drinking from the carry-out cans. Alan ordered Suzy to have sex with me on the carpet. As I undressed, I told Jill to take Alan's pants down and give him a blow job. I lay naked on a rug in front of a gas fire, clasped Suzy against my chest. I ran my hands down Suzy's back. Looked over to the sofa. Alan still had his shirt on but he was naked below the waist. Jill was running her tongue up and down his length. Alan was swigging from a can of lager and looking at me looking at him. I put my hands between Suzy's legs, she was wet. I fingered her clit, then slid a digit into her cunt. It was warm, it felt familiar, like an old friend. Suzy had an orgasm, then wriggled off my hand and went down on me.

I looked at Alan. He was excited. He removed his cock from Jill's mouth. He walked over to the fireplace and pulled Suzy's legs apart. She lifted her head and gasped with pleasure as he entered her. Then she lowered her head and licked my bits. Jill dropped her pants and hitched up her skirt. She walked over to me and sat on my face. I parted her beef curtains with my tongue. She was warm, moist and tasted of hyacinths. An orgasm exploded in the centre of my brain and rippled through my body. I was helpless, happy, falling. I was washing my face in Jill's moisture. Jill stood up. Alan was still fucking Suzy. Jill pulled Alan from his mount, pushed him face down on the floor, rolled him over. Guided Alan's erection between her moist lips, then started gyrating.

Karen came through from the bedroom, drowsy with sleep. She'd pulled on a dressing gown but was naked underneath. I told her to sit on Alan's face. She hesitated. I repeated the command, she did as I said. Suzy was still licking me and I had another orgasm as I watched Karen squat over Alan and then sink down. I was staring at the ceiling, drifting on a sea of words, the pattern in the carpet was reflected in the white paint glistening eight miles above my head. I was half-awake, the alcohol, the sex. I snoozed, woke up. Alan was leaving.

I told him to wait until I was dressed. I wanted to go with him.

We walked to the seafront. White foam, gulls whirling above our heads. Down on the beach we couldn't see the cafés or the esplanade that ran from them to the western edge of the sea defences. The smell of salt. Seaweed that was salt-encrusted. The ocean vast, heaving, amorphous. The white surf, lights of ships bobbing on the waves. White spray, surf, the roar of water forever rising and falling. I pressed a palm against my forehead. I felt all at sea. No longer knew who I was, whether anything separated me from that great mass of work. The ocean, the desert, inside outside, all around. What was I doing? I had to get away from the water. My mind spinning. I was in danger of falling. I mumbled something to Alan. We turned around, climbed up onto the esplanade. Saw that cars were still cruising up and down the strip. The Karens and Garys behind the windscreens were simulating a simulation, out-mything a myth. I found them more seductive than their elusive model, the film *American Graffiti*.

We trudged towards Union Street. Alan was talking about Erich Fromm again. He'd read through several Fromm books the previous night. They offended him. He'd sell them as soon as he could. Alan ridiculed the treatment of the futurist movement in *The Anatomy of Human Destructiveness*. Jibed that Fromm falls behind his own premises. If one is going to use historical methods, then the influence of Bergson's vitalism must be traced through Sorel to the futurists. Even on his own terms Fromm was mistaken to equate futurism with death. Alan stumbled, resumed his speech, but he'd forgotten about Fromm. He was angrily dismissing what Louis J. Halle had to say in *The Ideological Imagination*. A terrible book. I couldn't follow the thread of his argument.

We hit the square at the bottom of Union Street but swung right. I was on automatic pilot as we ambled down King Street. I just wanted to get home, go to sleep. Alan was still with me, was now part of me. I fumbled with the keys. My room needed cleaning. I lay down on the bed. Alan picked up my copy of *The Traveller Gypsies* by Judith Okely. He read a few pages, snorted derisively, picked up another book. Threw down the novel after reading the first paragraph. Retrieved Okely. Cambridge 1983. I closed my eyes, not sure if I was awake or asleep. Alan spent several hours examining my books.

That night I dreamt I journeyed from London up the A12. Then I was driving through Suffolk along really narrow country roads. Alan had sent me to stay with Dudley, his ventriloquist's dummy. Dudley made our tea with the things I'd brought from a bakery in Golders Green – begels with cream cheese, then *chokla* with jam. It reminded me of childhood holidays with my grandparents in London. I'd get to eat *chokla* as a treat at the weekend, after being made to eat black bread all week. I liked my grandparents and I liked London but I missed the South Coast. Dudley liked coffee, so we drank espresso with the bagels, but I insisted on making a pot of tea to wash down the *chokla*.

In my dream Dudley was an emaciated version of Alan. I found him very attractive. We hit it off right from the start. We talked about all sorts of things: music, films, books. Later on we went down to the beach. We could see the Sizewell nuclear power station at the end of it. We sat down and watched the waves rolling in as the sun set. We had the beach all to ourselves and although it was warm, I pressed myself against Dudley. Soon we were in each other's arms, rolling around on the pebbles. It wasn't long before my jeans were around my ankles and Dudley had his face buried in my cunt. It was incredible lying there, the sound of the ocean pounding in my ears and a vast expanse of thin cloud undulating in a darkening sky.

My cries disturbed some sea birds that had nested down for the night and many screeched angrily as they wheeled up towards the blackening horizon. Dudley was sucking my clit and working two fingers in and out of my hole. I wanted to feel the weight of his body pressing down against me, so I grabbed his ears and yanked hard. Dudley buried himself inside me. I could taste my love juice on his lips as they pressed against mine. Both Dudley and I were going crazy, shattering the peace of the night with our cries. Somehow I managed to tell Dudley not to come inside me. He kept fucking me, slowing down every now and then, until eventually he had to withdraw. I pushed Dudley onto his back, his jeans were still around his ankles, so I knelt to one side of him and ran my tongue up and down his dick. I'd enjoyed gazing up at the clouds, but I could see Dudley was staring at my arse, which was sticking up in the air.

Holding the base of Dudley's erection with my index finger and thumb, I took his fuck stick in my mouth. Having lubricated him with my saliva, I got a tad cruel. I clenched my teeth and ran them up and down his meat. Dudley squirmed beneath me, unsure about where to draw the dividing line between pleasure and pain. I repeated this trick several times, until the ventriloquist's dummy began screaming my name. Rolling it back and forth on his tongue. Anna. Anna. It was the same whichever way you said it. Backwards. Forwards. Anagramatised. Noon. Noon. I took one of Dudley's balls in my mouth and nipped playfully at the sack that contained them. A few minutes later I returned my attention to the dummy's shaft. It wasn't hard to get him to come in my mouth. My goal achieved, I French-kissed Alan's double. This gave me ample opportunity to spit the huge wad of spunk I'd extracted from Dudley into his mouth. I kept him pinned down until he'd swallowed it.

After that we just lay together on the beach for a very long time. We didn't think of taking a shower before we went to bed, we just wanted to collapse. We had sand all over us and after a bit more shagging, the bed was really gritty. We fucked some more in the tangled sheets when we woke. Then we headed for Saffron Walden. After parking the car we made our way into Bridge End Gardens. There was bird shit all over the benches in the park. Having squeezed through a piece of broken fence, we entered the Bridge End hedge maze from the east side. It took a lot of twisting and turning before we found our way to the centre. The statues and other monuments that originally decorated the maze had been removed. We made love at the goal and at this point I woke.

TWO

I AWOKE suddenly from the dark pool of sleep, Alan was already stirring, slipping out from between my floral duvet and a white sheet. It took me a while to remember who Alan was. I could hear him pissing into the toilet as I put the events of the previous day into place. When Alan re-entered my bedsit I laughed because he hadn't dressed and I knew that would have given the nymphomaniac who lived opposite me quite a thrill if she'd run into him on the stairs. Then I saw Hannah, my sex-mad neighbour, following Alan through the door. Hannah liked group sex and when she brought a bloke home who I found attractive it wasn't unknown for me to join in.

Alan stood above me grinning. Hannah embraced him from behind. Her hands snaked around his torso and she stroked his cock into an erection, then held it tightly. Hannah put the index finger of her free hand into her mouth and proceeded to massage saliva into Alan's left nipple. He squirmed with pleasure. I sat up and took Alan's cock in my mouth. Hannah sank to her knees and began to rim him. As I lubricated the length, I could feel myself getting all wet. I got onto my knees and turned around, so that Alan could enter me from behind, standing up. Hannah removed her skirt and panties, then climbed onto the bed. She pushed my head down against the mattress and clambered onto

15

my back, lying with her back against my back and her legs swung over Alan's shoulders.

I couldn't see anything, my eyes were closed but I knew from the sounds and movement of our bodies that Alan was licking Hannah out as he gave me a shafting. I came as Alan shot his load into my hole and from the way she screamed, I knew an orgasm had washed through Hannah's body too. There was a tangle of limbs and Hannah struggled up. Told us she had to rush or she'd be late for work. Alan crawled into bed beside me and we slept for the best part of two hours. We made love when we woke up. The missionary position, nothing exotic. Eventually we dressed. I was out of milk so we went to Carmine's on Union Terrace for an early lunch. Over pasta and cappuccinos we discussed literature.

Alan commented on my collection of Kathy Acker's work – *Great Expectation*, *Blood and Guts in High School*, *Don Quixote*, *Literal Madness*, *Empire of the Senseless*, *Portrait of an Eye*, *In Memoriam to Identity*, *My Mother: Demonology*, *Hannibal Lecter My Father*, *Bodies of Work*, *Eurydice in the Underworld* and *Pussy, King of the Pirates*. Alan admired Kathy Acker but said he could never read through to the end of her books. He was surprised when I told him I just read passages at random, it made no sense to read Kathy Acker from beginning to end. At some point Alan told me that in her essays Acker fell behind the premises from which she started out in her fiction. I told Alan he didn't know how to read. Imagine starting on page one with a book and then proceeding through to the end.

I'd heard stories about a number of the male writers Kathy lived with at varying times in her life. They tended to be less talented and less successful than Acker. It is alleged that one of these writers convinced himself that he was Kathy Acker while she was away on a promotional tour.

When Kathy returned home, the young writer was unable to sustain the fantasy that he was a successful novelist and suffered a nervous breakdown. Alan didn't think the story was true. It sounded suspiciously as if it was a fragment culled from a post-modern novel. Besides, Kathy was too cryptic to be involved in something so obvious. He began talking about Michael Bracewell, who I'd always thought of as a journalist. Alan produced three Bracewell novels from his bag. He told me Kathy Acker discovered Bracewell and took him to Serpent's Tail, who published his first book.

Alan explained that Bracewell was one of the first style or club novelists, an achievement that should be placed in the context of the long history of fiction aimed at teenagers. I still have three of Alan's Bracewell books and by looking through them I've been trying to piece together what he said over pasta at Carmine's. You can see from the books that Bracewell learnt to write as he went along. The prose style in *The Crypto-Amnesia Club* and *Missing Margate*, both dating from 1988, is quite atrocious. By the time *Saint Rachel* was published in 1995, Bracewell was producing chiselled prose in the mould of Aldous Huxley or Evelyn Waugh. Regardless of whether one likes the traditional English novel, it is still possible to appreciate the way Bracewell transformed himself into a prose stylist.

It is difficult to imagine Kathy Acker liking *Saint Rachel*, although Lynne Tillman admires it. Kathy would have liked everything bad about Bracewell. The flash. The coy iconoclasm of *Missing Margate*, which becomes a gender-bender novel when read alongside *The Fountainhead* by Ayn Rand. The way in which Bracewell's nostalgia for an England that never was allowed him to be seduced by everything post-modern. Those are the things Acker would have liked about Bracewell. Alan made the point that Bracewell's tragedy was that he'd learnt to write. The future was always leaking back and influencing the past. Having written competent works, Bracewell could never operate beneath the threshold of critical opinion.

The 80s ended in economic depression and while Bracewell's early work was marketed as satire, it was ultimately a celebration of middle-class consumerism. Everything had gone wrong and as *Saint Rachel* documented, it ended in Prozac. Bracewell's flaw was being more intelligent than Cyril Connolly. He knew from the beginning that he was a bad patriot, that the England he lusted after never had and never would exist. Bracewell was fixated on Englishness but his works described a different country from the land inhabited by the working-class heroes celebrated in best-selling books like *England Away* by John King. Bracewell came from Sutton and he overcame this lower-middle-class environment through celebrations of upward mobility.

In re-inventing himself Bracewell had to think through all the moves required to pass as completely bourgeois. The simulacrum was almost perfect but he lacked the arrogance and sheer stupidity of Anthony Powell. The broken relationships endlessly documented in Bracewell's novels function as signifiers of his broken dreams. He was a pastoralist even when he wrote about the city. Bracewell's second 'major' work was first published as part of *The Quick End* – works by three young novelists. When the time for reprinting came around, Don Watson and Mark Edwards were dropped and *Missing Margate* came out on its own. Bracewell was an 80s novelist. He lives on in journalism and TV appearances. Hotels, restaurants, designer clothes, a life-style organised around these objects of desire could never be sustained on royalties earned from moderately successful novels.

Bracewell had to fail in order to succeed. He'd a good reputation but hadn't amassed the sales to justify 20-grand advances. It was the media that provided him with the readies to sustain a middle-class life-style. Many writers are tempted by the money to be made from journalism. Bracewell was smart, he didn't strip-mine his subconscious by churning out confessional columns. Five-thousand-word features in the broadsheet press became his speciality, his name still carries connotations of quality. Bracewell hasn't embarrassed those literary figures who backed him early on, he isn't a Colin Wilson or Iain M. Banks. His early publishers are still proud of him.

The 80s have disappeared, most of the writers from that era are more or less forgotten. If Bracewell's work as a novelist is compared to the musical achievements of Duran Duran or Culture Club, his fellow travellers in a decade that style forgot don't even rank alongside the likes of Sigue Sigue Sputnik. Alan specifically mentioned John Wilde in relation to this. A hack like Wilde could only be compared to a band that never made it, a name that meant nothing. Having travelled in Bracewell's wake, the best a scribbler like Wilde could hope for was an afterlife interviewing burnt-out celebrities, a freelance fantasy without beginning or end. Wilde was voodooed, hexed, left trapped in the very nightmare Bracewell successfully escaped through acts of bewitchment.

Alan wanted to play a prank on Suzy. He called her from a pay phone and got himself invited to her pad. I had to round up a bunch of people Suzy knew. Suzy lived near the campus and loads of students passed her first-floor flat when they were making their way into the centre of town. Alan explained to Suzy that he'd always wanted to have sex with a woman while she leant out of a window conversing with her friends. Suzy was up for it. Alan kissed and cuddled Suzy, then took her knickers down and fingered her clit. Once the juice was really flowing, Suzy leant out of the flat to see who was in the street. I was talking to Jill beneath her living-room window. Suzy greeted us and asked us what we were doing. I explained that we were discussing Iain Sinclair's novels and that we both thought the deliberate ambiguity in his prose had close affinities with Andy Warhol's pop art.

Suzy was leaning out of the window, net curtains splayed down her back. I couldn't see Alan but I knew he had Suzy's skirt around her waist and that he was humping away. I'd arranged for a great many of Suzy's friends to wander down the street and soon there was a crowd of 20 people talking to her. Suzy's face was flushed and her conversation was incoherent. Suzy didn't like Michael, the guy who lived above her because he played Bob Dylan albums late at night. Michael was in one of my classes at the university and I'd rung him before Alan and I headed our separate ways. Michael had agreed that once a crowd of us had gathered in the street, he'd go and knock on Suzy's door. Alan whispered to Suzy that he'd deal with the caller. He walked out of the living room and into the hall. Alan adjusted his clothing, then let Michael into the flat.

Suzy didn't know it was Michael when he took Alan's place behind her. Michael had always fancied Suzy and was glad of a chance to fuck her. Suzy was trying to hold a conversation, so she wouldn't have noticed the change of rhythm when the two men switched places. Alan made his way onto the street and joined our group. He looked up at Suzy, greeted her and asked if she remembered him from the previous night. Suzy did a double take, her face a mask of confusion. Then she screamed. After Suzy came Alan explained the trick he'd played on her and with Michael still humping away this provided sufficient stimulation to give my friend a second orgasm.

Suzy invited everyone up to her flat and got the guys present to gang-bang her. I was up for having an orgy but

Alan restrained me. He insisted that it was Suzy's turn to be the centre of attention and that I shouldn't deny her this moment of glory. Alan was going through Suzy's books, she didn't have that many but he was impressed when he came across a copy of the *Selected Political Writings of Rosa Luxemburg*, edited by Dick Howard and published by the Monthly Review Press. This was 'a radical America book' from way back when in 1971. Likewise, Alan was amused when he discovered that Suzy had a copy of *I Love Dick* by Chris Kraus. This book incoherently documents the author's sexual obsession with Dick Hebdige, an English academic who was an intellectual celebrity during the 80s on the strength of *Subculture: The Meaning of Style*.

Subculture was Hebdige's first book and it was published in 1979, at a time when students still thought a polytechnic lecturer incredibly hip if he could talk about youth culture. Alan had to explain this to me because by the time I went to university every campus boasted its resident experts on the subject. Alan was amused that 20 years down the line Hebdige was being consumed as an object of desire rather than an expert on consumer fetishism. Alan found trends in academic publishing an endlessly absorbing topic and once he'd had his say about Hebdige, he moved on to Judith Williamson. Either then or later I argued with Alan when he insisted that the true value of *I Love Dick* lay in the way it exposed the misery of academic life and dished the dirt not only on Dick Hebdige but also on the likes of Felix Guattari and Toni Negri. I insisted the section on Hannah Wilke was the most useful thing in *I Love Dick*, although I also appreciated it as a parody of post-modern theorising. Once all the guys present had given Suzy a shafting, someone suggested we go down the pub. People began to leave, drifting off in different directions.

Alan wanted to sell some of his books, so we headed

to his place on Union Grove to collect them. Alan's flat looked pretty much as we'd left it, a mess. He started throwing books around. Making piles of first editions. Shuffling paperbacks. He kept turning over works by Jean Baudrillard as though they were trumps. He told me that he'd been rereading Bracewell because he was interested in the way psychoanalysis had transformed and retrenched 19th-century notions of characterisation and literary depth. From there he'd got onto an 80s kick. Leafing through the copy of *I Love Dick* by Chris Kraus at Suzy's place hadn't helped. Kraus was married to Sylvere Lotringer, who'd played a major role in translating, publishing and generally foisting Baudrillard on English-speaking readers during the 80s. *I Love Dick* was a down-market American equivalent of Baudrillard's *Cool Memories* where everything was allowed to hang out, including the fact that its author doesn't hack it as a writer of aphorisms.

According to Baudrillard everything had become transparent, obscene, there were no longer any secrets. Alan wasn't convinced by these claims, although Baudrillard doubtlessly provided Kraus and hipster hubby Lotringer with a theoretical justification for publicising their literary gang-banging. Alan didn't want to live after the orgy, he didn't even want to live out the death of the orgy, for Alan the orgy of history was without beginning or end. He wanted to deconstruct deconstruction. He wanted to sacrifice sacrifice. He wanted to seduce seduction and simulate simulation. He'd been reading Girard, Bataille, Marx, Hegel, Deleuze, Lukás, Hobbes, Virilio, Zizek and Irigarary. Alan wanted to be incoherent in his incoherence. The more he read the less he enjoyed reading. Derrida had been a huge disappointment. Having scanned Derrida's disciples, he needn't have troubled himself with *Of Grammatology*. He'd digested the contents before he consumed them, and after Derrida there seemed little point in rereading Rousseau or Lévi-Strauss. The more Alan read, the less he needed to read, it was an addiction.

I glanced at the ventriloquist's dummy sprawled across a chair and whispered his name. Alan picked up a copy of *Primate Visions: Gender, Race, and Nature in the World of Modern Science* by Donna Haraway and screamed as he threw it across the room. It was a big book, nearly 400 pages, and it dislodged several paperbacks from a shelf before clattering to the floor. Alan complained that he hadn't even started reading Judith Butler, let alone Donna Haraway. He probably didn't need to read either, since he'd devoured Sadie Plant's *Zeroes and Ones* in a single sitting, then flogged it. Where would he find the time for all this reading? It seemed as if he'd never stop living (the third section of *Baudrillard Live: Selected Interviews*, edited by Mike Gane is entitled 'I Stopped Living'; In *I Love Dick*, Chris Kraus claims that at the time she was stalking Hebdige he told her he hadn't read anything for two years). Was this the revenge of the crystal? Alan didn't know, it was all becoming too much. A French theorist like Baudrillard would be translated into English by some two-bit publisher like Semiotext(e) with minimal proofing and distribution, then before you knew it translations were spewing out from Verso, Polity, Pluto, Stanford and Routledge. Similar things had happened with Deleuze and Derrida, while Barthes and Foucault had become Penguin classics. You didn't need to keep up with it, you wouldn't want to keep up with it, you couldn't keep up with it.

Sometimes I wondered if what was going on between Alan and me was an exchange of subjectivities. The occasion of my second visit to his flat was the first time I got an inkling of this. Alan's world was becoming my world. Having read his Guattari, Alan wanted to become woman and in the process I felt like I was being transformed into a man. Why did I want to acquire all the books Alan possessed when they clearly hadn't done him any good? All Alan had learnt from his reading were more eloquent ways of explaining that he didn't know anything. He'd acquired cultural capital but at quite a price. It was a Faustian bargain that made no sense. It was an endless shuffling of texts and Alan was literally tripping over books in the process. There were paperbacks scattered across the floor. Alan tripped, I caught him. Alan's desperation to rid himself of these objects and simultaneously forget the words that ran through them was steadily increasing. The work was cut out for him. It was without beginning or end and that was where I came in. An alternative reading might be that Alan wanted to disappear, that he wanted to become an object. Since Alan had no religious beliefs he was unable to make a gift of his shadow to the devil and instead attempted to foist his subjectivity on me. Alan wanted to become a machine.

Alan showed me a yellowed newspaper cutting from the *Independent on Sunday* dated 21 July 1996. It was headlined 'Sinking In A Sea of Words: As academic journals proliferate, Noel Malcolm suggests dons write less, and think more'. At the end of the article a strapline acknowledged that the piece had been reprinted from the then current issue of *Prospect*. The gist of the essay was that academics were unable to keep up with their own specialised areas of research. Because career advancement was dependent upon publication, academics were forced to produce an endless stream of articles. The cutting suggested that on average an academic article has only five readers but didn't make clear whether this included the editor and two referees who were a standard feature of this part of the publishing industry. Alan wasn't even an academic and if specialists couldn't keep up with their own area of interest what hope was there for a general reader with interests across several fields?

The books Alan wanted to sell were double-bagged in carriers, then placed into a big rucksack. Although Alan had been kicking these books around his flat, as a good consumer he understood that he had to make it look like he cared about the crap he was off-loading. We didn't spend long at the Old Aberdeen Bookshop. Alan simply accepted the money he was offered. He didn't haggle. Once we were out on the street he'd said the price matched his expectation. Obviously he could have done better in London. While we were in the shop I bought a copy of *Stasi Slut* by Anthony Bobarzynski and now we were outside I gave it to Alan as a token of my affection. We walked down to the roundabout and Alan hailed a passing cab. We paid off the cabbie at Hazlehead Park, then went in search of the maze. Alan had read about it but this was his first visit.

The maze was locked up but the wire fence had been cut at the entrance and we pushed our way through the damaged barrier. It was a complex puzzle maze and we wandered back and forth for nearly an hour before reaching the goal. The hedge which formed the walls of the maze was in good condition and once we were at the centre we couldn't see anyone, although we could hear voices all around us in the park. I remembered the conclusion of my dream from the previous night. At that point I hadn't recorded it in my diary. I had to be careful, dreams are precious and easily forgotten. Alan had mentioned the Hazlehead Maze the previous day. I'd never heard of it and he showed me its entry in *The British Maze Guide* by Adrian Fisher and Jeff Saward. Since the book lists mazes alphabetically by place, Hazlehead, being in Aberdeen, is the very first entry.

In my dream I had sex with Alan at the goal of one of Saffron Walden's two mazes. I'd flipped through several books Alan possessed about mazes and had taken in various pieces of speculation connecting them to fertility rites. That and the rampant shagging I'd been engaged in no doubt accounted for the content of my dream. We were sitting on a park bench that had been painted green and placed at the centre of the maze. The colour alone was enough to suggest procreative rituals. I leant over Alan and fumbled with his flies. By the time I'd got his cock out of his pants it was erect. I went down on Alan, nipping playfully at his meat. I worked his length with my lips, tongue and teeth. There wasn't anything but the bench at the goal of the maze and I had no desire to experiment with sexual variations on the damp path, so I made Alan come in my mouth.

After Alan had adjusted his clothing we walked to a bus stop and chatted while waiting to get back into town. Alan was talking about novelists who deliberately set out to change their prose style with every book they wrote. Contemporary writers who did this tended to be viewed as wilfully perverse and while they'd achieve cult status among their fellow novelists, a broad readership would often prove elusive. Lynne Tillman was a case in point. Barry Graham was an equally good illustration. Graham's first novel *Of Darkness And Light* was a horror pastiche published by Bloomsbury. By the time of his third *The Book Of Man* he was being published by Serpent's Tail. This parodic retelling of the life of Alexander Trocchi carried endorsements from Irvine Welsh, Dennis Cooper and Lynne Tillman on the back cover. After that, Graham moved from his native Scotland to the USA, where he got Incommunicado to put out *Before*, which Alan perversely read as a heterosexual parody of Dennis Cooper. Alan hadn't read Graham's second novel and, given the way this author switched styles and themes, he had no way of knowing what it was like.

Thanks to our absorbing literary conversation, it didn't seem like long before we arrived at The Washington, a café on the seafront. I had egg, chips and beans. Alan hoovered up a cheese omelette with chips and peas. I drank coffee, Alan drank tea. Our tête-à-tête continued over this repast. Alan mentioned Lynne Tillman's *Motion Sickness* as an example of an anti-travel book. This was the first novel she'd had published in the British Isles. It had been preceded by *Absence Makes the Heart*, a collection of stories dating from 1990 that caused most English literary critics to write her off as a po-mo extremist. Tillman's first British publication came with back-cover endorsements from Harry Mathews, Gary Indiana and Edmund White. Her first novel *Haunted Houses* had been published in the US in 1987 with cover puffs from Kathy Acker, Edmund White, Harry Mathews and Dennis Cooper.

In 1992 Tillman published a collection of stories in the US under the title *The Madame Realism Complex*. This came out in the Semiotext(e) Native Agents Series, the editor of this series, Chris Kraus, would later publish her own work *I Love Dick* as a part of this list. While Alan admired all Tillman's work including her fourth novel *No Lease on Life*, he was particularly fond of *Cast in Doubt*. This novel featured two major characters, Horace and Helen. It was narrated by Horace, a gay man who wrote crime thrillers but hoped one day to complete a serious work. Horace might be taken as representing classicism or modernism. Helen, a young American girl who has disappeared, can be read as romanticism or post-modernism. The story is about Horace and Helen and the failure of the aesthetic formations they represent to find any point of contact. Helen is an absence in the text. It struck me that there was a feminist reading to be made of this but I said nothing. Alan paid for our food and we left the café.

We found a quiet pub with a decent selection of malts. Our plan was to make an imaginary tour of Islay by consuming whisky from each of its eight distilleries. I bought the first dram but before it was knocked back, Alan set the scene by describing a trip he'd made to the Hebrides. He began at Kennacraig, where he caught the ferry from the mainland. I was to imagine sitting on the deck with magnificent views to my left of the Kintyre peninsula, and on my right the Isle of Jura. The sun would be shining and fluffy white clouds scudding across the sky. Alan told me that it takes a little more than two hours to reach Port Ellen, a planned village of beautiful white houses laid out in 1821. The Port Ellen distillery has been closed for more than 20 years and the site is now used exclusively for malting. Fortunately, you can still buy Port Ellen whisky and Alan made me nose the malt before I drank it.

After we'd downed our first drink, Alan got up and ordered seven different malts, he brought the single shots back on a tray. The 14 glasses rattled as he placed them on our table. Alan had to be careful as he put down the drams, the whiskies had been lined up in the order we would drink them and he made sure they didn't slide out of their assigned places. Alan told me that the Laphroaig distillery is only a few minutes' drive from Port Ellen. I was to imagine walking from the public highway through the whitewashed distillery buildings to the sea. Laphroaig is a large distillery and from the seashore close to the visitor hospitality suite we would look across the water to the coast of Antrim, only twelve miles away. Like Port Ellen, Laphroaig has a peaty flavour but with a distinctive medicinal quality. I'd never been much of a malt drinker but Alan was converting me, I liked the fiery Islay flavours.

Our next stop was Lagavulin, just a short ride along the coast. Alan told me to imagine I was standing by the stream that runs through the distillery. By looking out onto a promontory I'd be able to see the ruins of Dunyveg Castle, the oldest parts of which dated from the 14th century. I nosed my malt then drained the glass. The amber fluid boasted an impressive heaviness, the taste was smoky and medicinal. Ardbeg was to be our last port of call on Islay's south coast, Alan told me to think of seals sunning themselves on the rocks close by this distillery. I nosed my shot and allowed it to sit on my tongue. I conjured up a tracking shot of the wildlife attracted to the wooded coastline that stretched up past the Victorian Kildalton Castle.

Our next dram was Caol Ila. The distillery is snuggled just along the coast from Port Askaig on the Sound of Jura. To get there we had to backtrack, since there was no direct route. We sped through Port Ellen and along the A846. The peatbogs flanking this remarkably straight road play a major role in giving Islay whiskies their distinctive flavour. We didn't stop in Bowmore, Alan said we'd return later, we simply sped on through Bridgend to Port Askaig. I was told a five-minute ferry ride to Feolin on Jura would provide me with the best view of Caol Ila. I was to picture the boat putting out, then imagine looking back at Islay and seeing the distillery just north of the ferry terminal. Once I was off the ferry, I was to climb up to the track that runs from Feolin to Inver. Looking across the Sound would provide a perfect view of the distillery with the sea shimmering in the foreground. The malt was less smoky than those from the south of Islay but still highly enjoyable.

Alan had been to Craighouse, eight or so miles from Feolin, the main settlement for Jura's 200 inhabitants and hence home to the island's whisky stills. However, he wasn't a fan of the whisky produced at the Jura distillery and since it wasn't an item on our fantasy itinerary, we

simply caught the ferry back to Port Askaig. The road
north to Bunnahabhain was frighteningly narrow. Alan
said he would park the car in the shoreside car park close
to the distillery, then we would wander north along the
coast before turning west. We'd cut across the north tip
of the island, a two-hour trek each way with no roads to
spoil the view and hundreds of deer all around us. On the
way back, we'd get a brilliant view of the distillery with
the Paps of Jura dominating the landscape from across the
Sound. As I nosed and then drank my Bunnahabhain I was
beginning to feel tipsy.

I imagined I was falling asleep in the car as Alan doubled
back through Port Askaig and Bridgend. I was tired after
our long walk. The Bowmore distillery was in the centre
of a planned village of the same name. Despite being on
a sea loch, Bowmore is the psychogeographical – as well
as the administrative – centre of Islay. A single Bowmore
Legend was my seventh successive dram and my palate was
shot to pieces. Alan's imaginary journey followed its own
logic, a serious whisky drinker would have concluded with
the heavier malts from the south of Islay, we had started
with them. Alan told me to picture doubling back once
again to Bridgend, then instead of heading for Port Askaig,
we'd follow the road around Loch Indaal to Bruichladdich.
This is the most westerly distillery in Scotland and after I'd
downed my dram, we left the pub. Alan wanted to go home
alone and read. Before we parted he gave me a copy of *69
Things to Do with a Dead Princess*, saying he'd like to know
what I thought of it. I made my way to King Street, had a
bath and took to my bed.

THREE

IN MY dream I was flying and then I was running along tracks. I was the Vienna-to-Belgrade express train. I collapsed into human form as the train pulled into Budapest. The station was old and had been conceived on a grand scale but the roof was smashed and dirty. I alighted from the train and Dudley the ventriloquist's dummy was waiting for me on the platform. We ran a gauntlet of impoverished Hungarians offering cheap accommodation before we finally made it out through the subway and onto the street. It was sunny and Dudley was using a 1989 edition of *Hungary: The Rough Guide* to find his way around town. All the street names had changed since the book had been published and it thus provided us with a wonderfully disorientating psychogeographical experience.

It was three hours since I'd left Vienna and I felt famished. We ate in a restaurant just off Erzsébet Körút called Pizza Bella Italia. We ordered pasta. The waitress was young and flirted with all the male customers. The room was too small for the murals of Italian buildings and a blue sky with clouds to work effectively. A red rose and a yellow banana indicated the gender divide of the toilets. I made my excuses and watched from the street as the waitress engaged Dudley in animated conversation. I was studying graffiti on a door when Dudley caught up with me. He liked the picture of a nude woman with a speech bubble above her head that read

'GYERC EREZM AKARON AWYELK ED!!!' This was followed by a telephone number and what appeared to be a name.

We wandered through the back streets and booked into the International Youth Hostel on Andrassy at the Octagon. Then we headed up to the Müvéz to enjoy one of Budapest's traditional coffee houses. We sat at a table on the street. Cars thundered down the road. After paying for our refreshments we moved on to Café Mozart for a post-modern simulation of the coffee house experience. There was an enormous selection of drinks but rather than providing different types of coffee, the variations consisted in strength, amount of milk or cream and the addition of flavours. The waitresses were dressed up in 18th-century costumes and the murals on the wall represented aspects of old-time Vienna. Mozart melodies were being piped through concealed speakers. I should have pinched myself, then I'd have gained immediate release from this nightmare landscape.

After what seemed an eternity, we left Café Mozart and headed through the red-light district to a bar called The Blue Elephant. We drank cherry brandy, while the working-class clientele played chess, drank and sang. For our second drink, Dudley had Unicum, while I had a pear brandy. The tables in the bar were chipped, the whole place was in need of redecoration. Once it got dark we ventured out onto the street and there were plenty of girls around. I saw Dudley standing under a street lamp. He'd got himself up in drag. Since I'd geared up as a man, I said I wanted sex. Dudley got in my car and we drove to the river. I told him to give me a blow job. I could feel the dummy's hands undoing my flies and sensed his irritation as he searched for my cock. I took a hammer from the glove compartment and smashed it into Dudley's skull. There was blood everywhere. I dragged the body down to the water and threw it into the Danube.

I walked downstream to Gresham Palace, a huge building decorated with the face of Sir Thomas Gresham, the man who'd founded the stock exchange in the City of London. One of the bottom corners of the building was now occupied by Casino Gresham. I turned around and looked at the river. Dudley was bobbing about in the water close to the bank. I reached out and grabbed him. The dummy had been dressed in an 80s power suit and this was soaking. Someone had attacked the mannequin with a hammer or an axe and the head was badly damaged. I carried Dudley back to the youth hostel and placed him in a bunk. I was about to crash when the telephone woke me.

Alan wanted to meet up. I was sleepy and the conversation was confused. Through this semi-conscious fog it emerged that Alan didn't know my name. I was quite shocked. After all we'd been at it like rabbits for a couple of days. I insisted that he'd said my name when I'd met him in The Grill. He explained that he'd said afternoon. That's when I realised I'd misheard him. I told Alan my name was Anna Noon and he laughed. We arranged to meet in Pizza Express. Both Alan and I had garlic bread and side salads with our pizzas. We didn't have any trouble getting a table. We met at noon, before the lunch-time rush really kicked in.

I asked Alan what he'd been reading. Explaining that he'd been attempting to compare Bracewell's output with more recent club novels, he said *Deadmeat* by Q. *Deadmeat* had been marketed as pulp despite the author's obvious literary aspirations. Although Q appropriated crime-novel clichés such as a narrator who'd just got out of jail, the work made formalist use of cyber, record industry and cinematic conventions. There was a very deliberate deployment of repetition. For example, an appeal for information about a killer runs as a refrain throughout the book. Paul Gilroy had eloquently defended black British identities in *The Black*

Atlantic and other works, Q seemed to be extending this discourse. The varied inflections in direct speech was only one of the more obvious ways in which this interest manifested itself in *Deadmeat*. It should go without saying that Q's notions and experiences of what it was to be 'English' were very different from those of Michael Bracewell, as was what he considered to be hip.

Rather than looking for clarity in his reading, Alan sought confusion. Was the clubber Q aware of the earlier English writer also known as Q and did his appropriation of this moniker form part of a conscious critique of the racial codings to be found in traditional literary discourse? The 'original' Q, Arthur Quiller-Couch, was an establishment man. Educated at Oxford, Q went on to lecture in classics at his alma mater, was knighted and even elected Mayor of Fowey in Cornwall, his home town. As well as writing novels and poetry, the 'original' Q edited the *Oxford Book of English Verse* and produced a slew of critical works including *Studies in Literature* and *Charles Dickens and Other Victorians*. Alan wasn't sure if Q had been consciously chosen by Q or whether some other force had brought them together. These doublings left him all at sea. Alan was hedging his bets over whether the uncritical attitude towards cultural commodification in *Deadmeat* was ironic or merely a result of the author's inability to think through the implications of those experiences that had initially politicised him. Indeed, given that the book as an artefact had provided an early vehicle for perfecting the commodity form, Alan often doubted the advisability of using literature to criticise capitalism.

Alan was deeply puzzled by Q's depiction of the cyber vigilante in his novel. This criminal, on the loose in London, lynched his victims and turned out to be a black American cop. The cyber vigilante was killing paedophiles and the

narrator appears to approve of this. Given the racial connotations of lynching, Alan considered it completely unbelievable that a black American would choose this as a method
for disposing of paedophiles. It didn't even seem credible
that the black British narrator of *Deadmeat* would approve
of lynchings. Alan didn't understand what Q was trying
to do, he was confused. He didn't know whether Q was
using irony and ambiguity to implicate certain of his readers
in the perpetuation of a white bourgeois subjectivity, or
whether the narrative merely reflected the author's inability
to escape the dominant code. While double consciousness
doesn't protect you from the code, it certainly gives you
different perspectives from which to reflect upon it.

Over coffee Alan discussed *Deep Cover: An FBI Agent
Infiltrates the Radical Underground* by Gril Payne. The
author of this work narrates the process by which he
became disenchanted with his employer and thereby lost
his sense of identity. No longer a conservative or a radical,
Payne becomes a hostage to fortune, tossed about on the
seas of adversity and stripped of his sense of self.[4] Alan
viewed the book as a cautionary tale, a warning to those who
wanted to get involved in the murky worlds of intelligence
and counter-intelligence. Once Alan had paid the bill, we
hit Union Street for a quick fix of commodity fetishism. I
bought lipstick and a new pair of shoes. I dragged Alan into
Waterstone's because I wanted to buy *The Lonely Planet
Guide to Iceland*. Bedtime reading that would take my mind
off my college work. We were thrown out before I could
make my purchase because an assistant spotted Alan rubbing
a pornographic novel against his crotch. Alan repeatedly
hissed the word 'bibliomania' as we were escorted from the
premises.

Alan had a backpack full of books and after I'd done my
shopping we trudged up to the Old Aberdeen Bookshop.

The proprietor wasn't in, so Alan left the books with his wife after arranging to return the next day when he'd be able to negotiate a price. Then we wandered down to the seafront and had a coffee in the Inversnecky Café. We were filling in time until Alan could pick up his car from the garage. A side window had been smashed by a thief who'd stolen some booze that Alan had left on the back seat. I announced that I felt like the narrator in Tania Kindersley's novel *Goodbye, Johnny Thunders*. Alan said he'd given up on the book at page 13 when the narrator described a man who'd shafted her as having politics to the left of Lenin. Alan thought that it was the job of novelists to deal with specifics not generalities. He'd wanted to know whether the shit in question was a Bordigist or a councilist, whether he favoured the politics of Rosa Luxemburg or Otto Rühle. Lenin had attacked the entire proletarian milieu in *Left-Wing Communism: An Infantile Disorder* and Alan snorted that it simply wasn't good enough to say that someone's politics were to the left of a right-wing reactionary.

I defended Kindersley, saying the whole point of her novel was its pointlessness. The story wasn't worth writing, a poor little rich girl playing at being bad and having a hard time getting over an affair with a complete loser. Besides, Kindersley clearly didn't intend readers to take her book seriously. No one was going to find characters whose musical tastes incorporated both Johnny Thunders and mid-period Pink Floyd in the least bit credible. The book was arch and ironic. It was futile to dismiss it as a complete waste of time. *Goodbye, Johnny Thunders* was aimed at avatars of boredom, individuals who were seeking out new ways to waste their time and found tedium comforting. It was a book for sad tossers who considered drugs both glamorous and dangerous. Alan didn't try to counter these claims. He just looked at his watch and paid for our cappuccinos. We chattered about monstrous twins as we made our way to the garage to collect his car.

I was disappointed when Alan's motor turned out to be a Fiesta. I'd expected something flasher. Still, it got us to Stonehaven, where Alan had located a photographer who was happy to take hard-core pictures of selected clients. I'd expected a bloke but it turned out that Alan had hired a woman to snap us in pornographic poses. Angela had tattoos and piercings but she was wearing baggy sportswear when she shot us making out on her waterbed and in her dungeon. It was all pretty clinical. Alan seemed to get off on it. I guess being a porn star isn't an unusual fantasy in our post-modern world. There were a whole set of routines Alan wanted to work through. Sucking, fucking and licking. He got extremely excited sitting on a chair with me perched on his lap, his cock up my cunt. Pure pornography. Alan insisted that the photographs of this pose should be taken full frontal with nothing hidden but the three-quarters of his prick buried inside me. This classic variation on a hetero-sexual theme proved to be the penultimate entanglement of the session. The last shot, predictably enough, was Alan coming in my face. The climax was fun but I didn't have an orgasm.

After we'd done Stonehaven Alan drove back to Aberdeen. In the car and over a light meal at Gerard's Brasserie we talked about books. Alan seemed to have William McGonagall on the brain. He had read *No Poets' Corner in the Abbey: The Dramatic Story of William McGonagall* by David Philips as well as the collected works of Scotland's alternative national bard. He knew a great deal more about McGonagall than I did at that time. McGonagall wrote doggerel but considered himself the equal of Shakespeare and Burns. He'd started life as a weaver but once the muse descended on him he endured 20 years of poverty as he determinedly followed the poet's calling. He was mocked and assaulted as he plied his trade in Dundee, pelted with eggs and rotten fruit during his readings. Indeed, his success as a buffoon was such that he was eventually hired to read nightly at a local circus but the disturbances whenever he performed became so riotous that he was banned by the local magistrates from appearing in public.

The upper classes in Edinburgh preferred to mock McGonagall in a gentler fashion. Feigning admiration for his would-be immortal works and paying handsomely for his entertainments. It didn't take the rich long to tire of McGonagall. They moved on to other things, leaving the poet to die in poverty. Alan considered many writers to be modern-day McGonagalls. The most perfect instance of this phenomenon was Joyce Cary. Obviously, *I Love Dick* by Chris Kraus elevated not only its nominal author but also her husband and collaborator Sylvere Lotringer to a similar status. Martin Amis fell into this category alongside all his scribbler friends. Sometimes it seemed as if there wasn't a living or recently deceased author who Alan didn't consider to be suffering from the McGonagall syndrome. Baudrillard remained one of Alan's favourite examples since no one could take seriously a man who accepted Sylvere Lotringer as his translator. According to Alan, all these hippie hipsters could think about was getting other men to shag their wives.

After our meal we drove out to the airport. Well, not really to the airport. We drove along the edge of an industrial estate behind the airport and then up a rough track, curving around a field. We'd arrived at Tyrebagger Hill and all we had to do to reach the recumbent stone circle situated on it was climb over a gate and cut across a field. Abandoned electricity pylons towered above us while a constant stream of planes and choppers soared into the sky from the airstrip below. Oil had made Aberdeen a busy airport. The stones were in a circle of trees and the site was extremely ambient. A surreal juxtaposition of ancient and modern. The airport, the industrial estate, the abandoned pylons and the stone circle. Alan claimed this combination was a killer. Real magic. No wonder K. L. Callan kicked off *69 Things to Do with a Dead Princess* with a visit to this site. Since I hadn't even looked at the book Alan had given me the previous evening, I didn't know what he was talking about. However I did think it a little strange that Alan weighed down his ventriloquist's dummy with bricks and carried it up to the monument. I didn't know Alan well, so I refrained from commenting upon his eccentric behaviour.

Recumbent stone circles are made up from a large stone on its side with two tall flanking stones, then a ring of stones radiating around this point of focus. The recumbent stone at Tyrebagger was tilted forward and there'd been a fire underneath it. The ash was stone-cold. Alan turned me around and made me kneel in it. Then my ride dropped his pants. His Levi's fell down around his ankles, his briefs only got as far as his knees. Alan had an erection. This didn't surprise me. He spread his arms and leant forward, balancing himself against the recumbent stone. I shook Alan's prick vigorously, then ran my tongue along its length. Alan groaned and the volume of his moaning increased when I sucked his cock into my mouth. I worked my lips gently up and down the shaft for quite some time and although Alan bawled his lungs out, he didn't come. I decided to use my teeth. The harder I chomped the more Alan writhed and screamed. As he came I could see a plane taking off from the runway beneath us. After this, we swapped places and Alan licked me out.

Eventually we got back in the car and Alan drove down to the airport. We went into the terminal and ordered cappuccinos from a concession called Deli France. Aberdeen has a disproportionate number of French-style eateries because people with money to burn seem to consider brasseries sophisticated. The service in Deli France was lousy, the coffee wasn't bad. After Alan made a purchase in the whisky shop we headed to the car. It only took 15 minutes to get back to the city centre. We high tailed it to Alan's flat. He got out a Polaroid and made me act out his sexual fantasies with the ventriloquist's dummy. The poses were pretty similar to those we'd struck in front of the professional photographer in Stonehaven. This time, however, books were obsessively rearranged on the shelves behind Dudley and me. Works by writers such as B. S. Johnson and Alain Robbe-Grillet were reordered as I threw generic pouts and acted out pornographic clichés in front of the camera. As he felt the sticky heat of the paperbacks with his palms, Alan told me that he found books extremely erotic. They made him want to shit in his pants.

After a while Alan threw the dummy across the room. He was feeling jealous. Then my companion started throwing books around. He tried to play football with *Aren't You Rather Young to Be Writing your Memoirs* by B. S. Johnson. All the while Alan ranted about the irresolvable ambiguity of Johnson's work. According to Alan, Johnson made such ridiculous claims for his prose that it was hard to believe anyone had ever taken him seriously. Johnson's theoretical explanation of his output fell behind the premises on which his work was based. Alan considered Johnson to be simultaneously tedious and hilarious. He began ranting about the publicity generated by Johnson's relationship with his mother, Johnson's desire for his mother to appreciate his books. Johnson's obsession with his mother. Alan denounced Johnson for Oedipalising literature. He bemoaned the fact that an incredible technical ability had been fettered by Johnson's strait-laced mind. Alan denounced Harry Mathews and Raymond Queneau for suffering from the same vice.[5] Then he announced that Georges Perec was the only OULIPO writer he rated. Eventually I got Alan to calm down. We had a dram, then retired to bed and had sex. Straight sex. Missionary position. Despite the fact that Alan was into virtually every erotic variation known to man, he always insisted that the highest of highs was post-coital sex. For Alan sex was primarily a mental phenomenon and he wished to exhaust himself with it.

That night I dreamt that we picked up Alan's Fiesta from the airport car park and drove through the night to the Cambridgeshire village of Hilton. The rosy fingers of dawn were breaking through the clouds as we walked across the village green, which was allegedly landscaped by Capability Brown. An ancient turf maze was our goal and we walked the nine circuits of this unicursal labyrinth to reach the William Sparrow monument at its centre. Retracing our steps, we made our way out of the maze and lay down on the green. One thing led to another and it wasn't long before we were making love in the dew. My pleasant dreams vanished and I awoke because the bed was shaking. I could feel hot breath on my face and I forced my eyes open. Alan was bending over the bed, adjusting the sheeting, he'd laid the dummy down beside me. I wanted to cry out but my voice caught in my throat. Moonlight was filtering through the undrawn curtains and I could see Alan's eyes, they were closed. He was sleepwalking.

Alan straightened up and left the room. Gingerly I lowered my legs over the edge of the bed. I followed Alan into the living room. He was shuffling books. Feeling the hot surfaces. Reading paperback tomes with his fingers. All the while reciting random lines corrupted from Shakespeare. Put out the light. Not all the perfumes of Arabia. I thought about waking Alan. Then I remembered I'd read somewhere that it can be dangerous to disturb sleepwalkers. I left him with his crime novels and went through to the kitchen to get a glass of water. By the time I'd slaked my thirst and returned to the living room Alan was gone. I found him in his bed embracing the dummy. I lifted the duvet and climbed in beside them. This woke Alan. Instantly awake, he unceremoniously tossed the dummy to the floor and embraced me. Our lips met, I could feel Alan's erection through my nightie.

Alan was in no rush to fuck me, he wanted to make sure I was properly lubricated before entering my cunt. So he ran his hands over my body, tweaking my nipples and teasing me by brushing his hands close by my quim without touching my clitoris. Alan was an experienced older man. I've never met anyone who made love with such scientific deliberation. Every stroke told to the uttermost. He slowly drew out his prick until the tip of the glans only rested between my lips, and then with equal deliberation drove it slowly back, making its ridge press firmly against the upper creases of my vagina as it passed into my cunt. Then when the whole length was enclosed and it seemed as if even my belly had been filled by it, Alan gently worked it about from side to side, causing the big round head to rub deliciously on the sensitive mouth of my womb. In my ecstasy I was bellowing obscenities. Then we both groaned with excess of pleasure, and my cunt tingled round his palpitating tool as the life flood darted from the opposite sources of delight in reciprocating streams of unctuous spunk.

Alan lay back to recover his breath and rest himself after these exertions. When he saw me wiping my wet receiver with a tissue, he asked me to perform the same kind office for him. I willing complied, and kneeling at his side took his soft and moistened prick into my hands and tenderly wiped it all round, then stooping forward I pressed my lips on its flowing tip. This position elevated my behind and Alan proceeded at once to avail himself of it. Throwing my nightie over my back, he moved me towards him until my naked posterior was almost opposite his face. Then spreading my thighs, he opened the lips of my quim with his fingers, played about the clitoris, and having moistened his finger in my cunt, pushed it into my arsehole. While Alan tickled the crannies and fissures of my backside, I fondled his prick and moulded his balls. After a while I straddled directly over him, then stooped until my sex rested on his mouth. I was dripping as I felt his warm breath blowing aside the hairs of my cunt, and his pliant tongue winding round my clitoris, playing between my nymphae and exploring the secret passage inside. When he went on to the nether entrance, and I felt the titillation of his tongue amid its sensitive creases, the sluices of pleasure burst open and I became conscious of a melting sensation.

I twisted my rump and expanded the wrinkles in my arsehole to let Alan's tongue further in. I took the head and shoulders of his prick into my mouth and sucked with all my force, screwing my tongue around its indented neck and all the while, moulding his balls with one hand and frigging his arse with the other. Alan began to heave his loins up and down, driving his manhood in and out of my mouth as if he were fucking it. His pole grew larger, stronger and hotter. I felt his open mouth in my cunt sipping up the pleasure drops that trickled down its excited folds. Finally, a torrent of hot spunk, luscious and sweet, burst into my mouth and flowed down my throat. I twisted around and soon we were asleep in each other's arms. I dreamt of crop circles, shooting stars and forbidden books. Alan whispered in my ears that he could never remember his dreams. I didn't believe him. He wanted to lose his subjectivity, wreak crystal revenge, but his fatal strategy hadn't reached fruition yet.

FOUR

CRAWLING UP slowly from a deep pit of sleep, my body pinned beneath Alan's weight. His chest pressing down against my back. Alan's cock between my legs as I negotiated the twilight zone between consciousness and oblivion. After Alan came he struggled up through tangled sheets. I could feel Alan's residue dripping between my legs. Alan left the door open and I heard him pissing. The sound of water being splashed on his face. When I heard the kettle boil I got up. I washed, dressed, made my way through to the kitchen. Alan threw a copy of *Intellectuals* by Paul Johnson onto the table and poured me a cup of tea from the pot. He made some cryptic comments about Johnson's career resembling that of a hack called J. C. Squire.

Alan didn't like Johnson's *Intellectuals*. He read out a passage from Marx that Johnson claimed was meaningless and then provided an exegesis. Alan didn't like writers who treated their readers as if they were morons. Johnson was providing an ultra-low-grade introduction to the works of everyone from Rousseau to Sartre, before proceeding to concentrate on what he perceived to be the sexual failings of his subjects. The chapter on Marx was typical. Johnson claimed the author of *Capital* was unable to sustain himself over the entire length of a book, but *Intellectuals* was simply a series of poorly drawn prose sketches that could be detached from each other without any alteration to their meaning. Rather than developing an argument, Johnson simply reiterated his irrational prejudice against critical thinking in a series of poorly schematised chapters. Johnson claimed that Marx was essentially Talmudic in his writings, that he 'merely' provided a critique of the work of others. The same argument could have been deployed against Johnson had he risen to the level of critical discourse. As for Johnson's sex life, the less said about that the better.

Alan got up and left the room. When he returned he handed me a copy of *Karl Marx: His Life and Work* by Otto Rühle. This tome, Alan explained as he fried some mushrooms, may have been marred by cheap psychologising but it had the merit of moving beyond the sterile arguments usually found in the prose of those who wanted to defend the work of Marx. Rühle was an influential left-communist who as far back as the 20s happily admitted Marx had personal faults galore. This, alongside texts such as *The Struggle against Fascism Begins with the Struggle against Bolshevism*, had made Rühle unpopular with right-wing reactionaries such as Lenin and Trotsky. Rather than attempting to defend Marx's personal failings, Rühle ingeniously claimed that these character flaws were what enabled the communist theoretician to carry out his important work on behalf of the proletariat.

Alan placed a plate in front of me. Spread across it were two slices of toast, one covered with beans, the other with fried mushrooms. Alan sat down at the other end of the table and we tucked into this fare. Once we'd cleaned our plates, Alan asked me whether I'd rather go to Dundee or Bennachie. At that point I didn't know that Bennachie was a mountain. Since Alan insisted I make a choice I decided to flip a coin. Once fate had directed us south to Dundee, Alan told me to examine the coin I'd grabbed from the kitchen window sill. I turned it over in my hands, both sides bore a head. Fate was pushing me in the direction of one of the least attractive towns in Scotland, which had been rebranded 'City of Discovery' by a local council desperate to attract tourists.

Once I'd belted up and we were heading out of Aberdeen over the Brig o' Dee, I found myself fiddling with the Fiesta's glove compartment. I opened it up and pulled out a stack of books, *Head Injuries* by Conrad Williams, *Cocaine Nights* by J. G. Ballard, *Perfumed Head* by Steve Beard, *Come* by Mark Waugh ('CD limited edition' with the CD detached from the package) and *Been Down so Long It Looks Like up to Me*, 'the classic novel of the 1960s', by Richard Farina. We were speeding down the A90 with Portlethen flashing by on the left. I didn't know it then, but there were a number of impressive stone circles just to our right, at least one of which is visible from the road. I asked Alan about the books. He said he'd been meaning to dump them at the Old Aberdeen Bookshop. I could tell Alan was in a bad mood, he was usually more reticent about broadcasting his opinions but that morning he was indulging himself with a torrent of abuse. I guessed, incorrectly as it turned out, that Alan would have preferred Bennachie to Dundee as a destination.

Farina, Alan informed me, was a complete bummer, the worst kind of hip writing you could imagine. Leonard Cohen on downers. The Ballard didn't have a lot to recommend it either, a late work where every concession was made to outmoded literary motifs such as characterisation. Alan said he'd heard it argued that *Cocaine Nights* was Ballard's attempt at camp, the author was simply sending himself up, parodying both his own work and that of more conventional novelists. Alan didn't buy into this theory. A bad book was a bad book was a bad book. *Cocaine Nights* bristled with middle-brow clichés including an opening sequence that did little more than establish the narrator as a travel writer. Ironically, the hero swiftly abandons this pursuit and takes up the management of a leisure club. Described baldly, this sounds as if it must be parody but Alan assured me that the words simply fell dead from the page. No wonder the book had been shortlisted for the 1996 Whitbread Novel Award.

Alan was damning about *Head Injuries* too. He called it reactionary. Conrad Williams was a young writer specialising in what enthusiasts describe as spectral fiction. Basically this meant a horror novel with literary aspirations. Its protagonists were lonely and Williams explores their past and present lives in the kind of tedious detail that could only appeal to retards who appreciate 'literary depth' and 'characterisation'. The book's primary redeeming feature was the way Williams kept the explanation of what was happening open, so that the reader was forced to make their own choice between a psychological and a supernatural explanation.

Alan was considerably more enthusiastic about *Come* and *Perfumed Head*. Both dispensed with a linear plot, which was something Alan always appreciated in a contemporary novel. While experimental fiction had been popular in the 60s and 70s. with a temporary waning of revolutionary contestation and the ongoing conglomeration of the publishing industry, editors had become increasingly conservative and most of those based in the British Isles viewed non-linear fiction with complete disdain. Experimental writing was rarely published, and the few works of this type that did appear inevitably came out on independent presses. *Come* and *Perfumed Head* would find their readers over time precisely because they transcended the times at which they were produced.

A ring road looped us around the suburbs of Dundee,

then suddenly we were parking on Union Street with the silvery waters of the Tay Estuary almost visible a few hundred yards to the south. Alan had the keys to a flat on the west side of the street. We climbed the stairs and found ourselves inside Pete Horobin's Data Attic. Horobin was an artist who during the 80s documented every aspect of his life: what time he got up, went out, who he met. He even recorded when he had a shit. The records of this activity were stored in the flat in notebooks and on data sheets. Every day for ten years Horobin had stencilled the date on a sheet of paper and then attached a photograph or some other memento of the hour. Horobin claimed that he was breaking the creative process into its constituent parts but the results actually came across as a Kafkaesque bureaucracy gone mad.

Visiting the flat gave me an inkling of what those who'd discovered the *Marie Céleste* must have felt on boarding that deserted ship. Horobin had saved everything he'd used during the 80s. The flat was full of worn-out shoes and clothes, not to mention the packaging of all the food he'd consumed. Give it 50 years and this stuff would be a gold mine, museums would be bidding millions for it. But until it attained rarity it was just worthless junk. Horobin had disappeared, allegedly in the direction of the North Pole. Although he'd been unemployed for most of the ten years of the project, Horobin had somehow managed to buy the place. I never did discover why Alan had access to the flat or who covered the bills for its missing owner.

The aesthetic madness of the Data Attic contrasted sharply with the chaos of books that overflowed Alan's flat in Aberdeen. Horobin's detritus was ordered, everything was catalogued and put away in its place. Still it made little sense for someone to fill their pad with junk even if they wanted to create a time capsule. Alan, of course, considered this total environment to be far more sinister than an ascetic expression of taste. The Data Attic was Pete Horobin's way of imposing his consciousness on others. It was the means by which he intended to inject his subjectivity into receptive young minds. I don't know whether Alan was attempting to impress me or distract me. Behind the flat was a block of offices and I was keen to have sex in the back bedroom because I knew scores of white-collar workers would be able to watch me as I undressed.

Alan dropped his trousers quite unselfconsciously. He frigged himself and told me to get my kit off. I half-heartedly resisted these entreaties and found myself wrestling Alan on the bed. After much laughing, dragging and pushing, Alan succeeded in getting his hand on my chink of delight. I enjoyed watching his face beam with satisfaction as his eager fingers felt the swelling mound and soft, rounded lips which formed the outer portion of my sex. Alan praised and kissed me. Pressed hard against me. He pinched my clitoris and his fingers rubbed my slit, as he softly pulled up my frock and pulled down my M&S knickers until I was at last exposed in the way he desired. Alan positioned me on the bed so that any of the desk jockeys who cared to look could get a full view of my delights.

Alan's eyes sparkled when he kissed the lips of my cunt and then thrust in his tongue. He was leaning over me on one side, so I let my hand stray up his thigh. Alan's prick stiffened as my fingers closed around it. He seemed greatly pleased and lifting himself up, he pushed it forward towards my face. I began to frig the erection, all the while keeping my gaze fixed firmly on the prick. Alan asked me to give him a blow job. I took his manhood in my mouth and twined my tongue around it. Alan moaned and I sucked. As I pulled myself free and told Alan to shove his dick up my slit, I noticed that a number of office workers had abandoned their tasks and were gazing at us through the bedroom window. Knowing I had an audience got me excited and it wasn't long before I'd come. I let Alan bang away for a few minutes, then pushed my grinding partner onto his back and jerked him off.

Adjusting my clothing I gazed out of the window. White-collar workers busied themselves at their computers, studiously avoiding my gaze. Alan smoothed the bed sheets, determined to leave the flat exactly as we'd found it despite the fact that its owner was unlikely to return. I was given a lightning tour of Dundee city centre. Bland pedestrianised streets giving access to some extremely ugly shopping malls. The Hilltown had more ambience but despite its position on rising ground and general aura of attractiveness, this area proved incapable of dominating the city's psychogeography. From the Hilltown the visit to Dundee concluded with a sprint to the summit of Law Hill, then ten minutes at the top to take in the view. Returning to the car past the Nethergate Centre made me appreciate Aberdeen and its famous architect Archibald Simpson. My adopted home had succeeded in retaining some dignity in the face of ever-increasing commodification and a trend towards extremely tacky public art.

There was something Alan wouldn't address, perhaps couldn't address. Once we arrived at Edzell Castle I tried to get at it by asking him about his favourite books, a top ten or twenty. Alan was offended, he wasn't interested in giving his opinion or compiling lists since this was precisely the kind of banal response sought by market researchers and utilised in the mass media. We wandered amongst the box hedges in Edzell's formal garden, a renaissance masterpiece, disturbing pheasants who'd rush off into neighbouring fields. There were some really beautiful emblems carved into the remains of the castle. I recorded that we took in Saturn, Jupiter, Mars, Sol, Venus, Mercury and Luna. Alan's mood improved and I knew I'd hit on something when I asked him about the writer K. L. Callan. My companion considered Callan's commercially published works to suffer from an excessive deference to literary aesthetics, but he rated the disgraced novelist's more eccentric and often self-published productions very highly indeed. In particular, and as I already knew, Alan was obsessed with a non-fiction work entitled *69 Things to Do with a Dead Princess*. I was to hear a good deal more about this text over the following days. But for now I must try not to jump ahead of myself. At this point I still hadn't read the copy of Callan's book that Alan had presented to me several days before.

Looking at my notes, I find it difficult to put every-thing together exactly as it happened. If memory serves me we drove via Fettercairn to the Clatterin Brig Restaurant. George and Ina, who run the place, offer big meals at low prices and their vegetarian dishes have the surreal quality of pub grub. My spring rolls came with sweet and sour sauce and rested on a huge bed of rice. This substantial platter was fleshed out with a hint of salad and a massive portion of chips.[6] From the Clatterin Brig we drove to the Grassic Gibbon Centre at Arbuthnott. Our indifference bordered on disdain as we viewed pens, coins and a dressing gown that had once belonged to the long dead hack writer Lewis Grassic Gibbon.

Rather than heading directly home from Arbuthnott we took in the beach at Inverbervie. Our next stop was a Templar kirkyard at Maryculter. We weren't banging about Deeside because Alan was interested in the royal connection. His obsession with Maryculter had developed after he'd read *The Temple and the Lodge* by Michael Baigent and Richard Leigh. At least this is what Alan told me. However, when it came to discussing books Alan plainly enjoyed making ambiguous statements. One might have taken what Alan had to say about Baigent and Leigh as praise, but as I became increasingly familiar with his modus operandi I realised that his pronouncements on the more outlandish theories concerning Freemasons were a not-so-subtle brand of satire.

The kirkyard was walled and situated immediately behind a country hotel. There wasn't another human being in sight when we arrived. Alan's hand went around my waist and he pressed me in his arms. He kissed my cheek. He kissed my lips. My imagination was inflamed as Alan's toyings became bolder. His hands went under my blouse and my breasts were brought to light. As Alan waxed warmer I grew increasingly languid and yielding. He lifted my skirt and exposed to view my fleshy thighs and the rich tuft of hair which nestled at a voluptuous angle at their junction. He pushed me onto my back and after whipping off my knickers, pulled my legs apart. Then Alan parted the soft, moist folds of my skin with his fingers. He pressed his middle finger into my love passage and I squirmed with delight. Before long, Alan's finger had been replaced by his cock. He plunged in and a shiver of delight passed through my frame. We both came quickly. It took only a few moments to adjust our clothing and depart.

I remember that after leaving the graveyard we went into the Maryculter Hotel and had coffee. Alan paid, and if I recall correctly I was horrified by the price. In retrospect it is very difficult to place everything in order, my own memories have become confused with things Alan told me and incidents I read about later in his books and diaries. I'm sure we went into the kirkyard before going into the hotel but I'm not sure whether we hit Maryculter before Portlethen. Anyway, at some point before heading back to the Granite City, we visited four stone circles to the west of Portlethen. Craighead Badentoy was our first stop. This much-disturbed four-poster belonged to people running dog kennels. We knocked at the door and once all the dogs had been brought in from the field we were given a tour of the stones by a very friendly woman. The circle had a nice feel to it, the raised bank making it particularly enticing as a location for an outdoor shag – although there was little chance of having sex at the site given that most of the time it was overrun by dogs. After thanking our guide for sharing her knowledge of the site with us, we walked down the hill and through an industrial estate to Cairnwell. This is a Clava ring cairn that has been moved a few hundred yards to provide a feature on an otherwise featureless industrial estate. Alan carried Dudley on his back to both these circles.

Having retrieved the car, we backtracked to Auchquhor-thies, only a mile and a half from Craighead Badentoy. At some point we made love under a waning moon at this monument. As far as I can recall our first visit to this recumbent stone circle was made while it was still light. We didn't bother asking the farmer's permission to go into the field since Alan generally preferred to trespass. The circle was comprised chiefly of red stones although the recumbent and the one remaining flanker were of quartz-streaked granite. A mere 300 yards away was Old Bourtreebush, and all we had to do to get to this badly damaged circle was cross a field. It was while traversing the field between these two ancient monuments that I began a series of ongoing conversations with Alan about horror and slasher films. Alan was fascinated by low-budget celluloid of the 70s and 80s, not simply because he'd grown up watching this trash, he was morbidly obsessed with the way their mainly male audiences identified with female victim-heroines.

I remember one time I went out to Old Bourtreebush with Alan's ventriloquist's dummy and it might have been the books I'd been reading, but I ended up dressing the dummy in garlands of grass and trying to get a cow to eat it. Alan always carried the dummy around in the car and I guess we had it with us that first time we headed out to Auchquhorthies. Anyway the cows wouldn't eat the dummy despite the fact that it was dressed in a fine suit of grass. Alan said cryptically that I'd end up eating him. Or perhaps this was when I first declared my intention to make a meal from Alan's mortal remains, or at least began planning to do just that. I'm jumping ahead of myself here but what Alan was doing to me with all his talk about books and subjectivity was like rape and in the end it more or less killed me. It wasn't that I wanted to murder Alan, the script simply made his death inevitable, that's the whole point of a rape-revenge narrative, the rapist has to die.

By the time we got back to the car, Alan was talking about a novel called *The Hackman Blues* by Ken Bruen. While Alan thought the book was competently executed, he wasn't interested in getting inside the mind of a psychotic criminal, particularly when the first-person narrator manages to constitute himself as a centred subject despite the fact that he'd been medicalised in a way that makes it clear he was highly resistant to bourgeois norms. A dog howled at the moon and Alan mentioned his real beef about Bruen's book. The narrator, who has zero taste when it comes to booze, at one point orders a Glenfiddich because he thinks it makes him sound as if he knows his stuff. Alan would have taken an Islay any day of the week. I think it was there and then in the car, as Alan ranted about Ken Bruen, that I decided I'd devote my middle years to a militant campaign aimed at the liberation of prostitutes.

Alan didn't bother asking the farmer's permission, we

just motored straight back to the Granite City. We weren't
travelling far, seven or so miles, and as he drove Alan told
me about a book he'd read by a guy called Peter Mason
called *The Brown Dog Affair*. It was a true and historical
account of a monument to a vivisected dog put up in
London in 1906. The statue was considered provocative
by reactionaries and its erection led to riots on the part
of medical students the following year. I couldn't really
fathom Alan's enthusiasm for the book and I still can't
although I have this self-published curiosity in front of me
as I write. From the heights of Portlethen the Granite City
was spread beneath us like silver on white linen. The view
reminded Alan of a book he'd once read called *A Grain of
Truth: A Scottish Journalist Remembers* by Jack Webster.
Alan chuckled about this old hack going completely over
the top as he described returning from Glasgow to his native
Aberdeenshire.

That evening we ate at Pacific Winds, which advertised itself as the most elegant and spacious restaurant
in Aberdeen. Chinese and Thai cuisine, telephone 01224
572362, 25 Crown Terrace, open seven days, lunch 12–2pm,
evening 5.30–11pm. All major credit cards accepted. We
both ate cashew-nut stir-fry under an enchanted moon.
Even more than the food, I savoured the welcome of
courteous service. Alan showed me a used copy of T. S.
Eliot's *Four Quartets* between the starter and the main
course. I remember reading the hand-written inscription
on the blank pages at the back of the book for the first
time in Pacific Winds, I've read it many times since: '18th
July 1961. This evening we sat on a semi-circular red sand
bin at Aldgate bus station waiting for a Green Line coach.
We read, Love ... ceases ...' I spilt coffee on the book
several years ago and most of the quoted lines of poetry
became unreadable due to smudging.

As we relished the pleasure of exceptional dishes and a soothing atmosphere of soft music, I still retained sufficient use of my critical faculties to realise that there was nothing startlingly original about Alan's claim that T. S. Eliot was a reactionary. Likewise, it wasn't difficult to see why Alan felt he'd been raped when bourgeois culture had been forced upon him during the course of lessons at the London secondary school he'd attended. Alan felt it was wrong to repress memories of abuse, he wanted to understand what had happened to him, why he'd been the only boy in his class to make it all the way to university. Alan had been raped by those who'd forced him to constitute himself as a bourgeois subject but his tormentors had been similarly abused.

That night, or one night before or after it, I refused to let Alan into my bedsit. I was embarrassed. I wanted to hide the evidence of abuse. Alan didn't know I'd been buying up his unwanted books as he flogged them to the Old Aberdeen Bookshop. I got into the habit of taking the books to the shop for him. Actually, I'd just take his fraying carrier bags straight to my place. Cut out the middle man. I was a gender bender. Adopting a bourgeois sensibility not only made me a centred subject, I was simultaneously coded white and male. As a teenage girl I'd had a fetish for snakes but Alan gave me a fetish for books. I liked the smell of them, old and musty, I liked to cup them in my hands as I took a shit. I no longer let Alan come around to my place. The shelves in his pad were emptying. He was beginning to tear out the wood and metal brackets supporting them. I took the shelving when I could. Re-erected it in my bedsit. Books were piling up on the floor. Towers of books were piled up against the walls. There were books jammed under my bed. I wanted to possess Alan by possessing everything he'd ever read.

That night I curled up with a copy of *The Essential*

Frankfurt School Reader, edited with introductions by Andrew Arato and Eike Gebhardt. I fell asleep reading an essay by Theodor W. Adorno entitled 'On the Fetish Character in Music and the Regression of Listening'. I was neglecting my studies, I preferred to read Alan's books. *The Essential Frankfurt School Reader* was a compromise. It had belonged to Alan but would help me with my course work. The green spine was faded and badly scored. I bought the tome for £5.95 from the Old Aberdeen Bookshop. The price was pencilled onto the flyleaf. The original price sticker was still on the back, £6.60 Net BASIL BLACKWELL. I was certain Alan hadn't bought the book new and wondered how much he'd paid for it.

I slept uneasily. I dreamt that the towers of books piled up around me came crashing down onto the bed, crushing me. I died and Dudley strode into the ruins of my room dressed in a fireman's uniform. The dummy sifted purposely through the wreckage, eventually locating my body under multiple copies of *69 Things to Do with a Dead Princess.* Then Dudley sodomised me. After shooting his load into my rotting rectum, he took a big bite out of my buttock. The dummy became increasingly excited as he slapped my dead flesh and called me hundreds of insulting names. Slut. Harlot. Trollop. Arsewipe. Turd burglar. Shirt lifter. Brown nose. Dudley spread me across the bed, carefully parting my legs as he did so. Then he took a straw from behind his left ear and shoved it inside me. The dummy pushed the straw into my bladder and sucked out urine. He was taking the piss. Being inanimate himself, Dudley thought it was funny that I was dead.

FIVE

I DON'T remember when I woke up or where I met Alan. However, I do know that I'd been up to his flat on Union Grove before we drove out to the Maiden Stone at Bennachie. Alan was angry that I hadn't let him sleep with me the night before. I was embarrassed, my bedsit was overflowing with the books he'd been selling. At first I'd just been buying them from the Old Aberdeen Bookshop. Then I'd hit on the idea of offering to take them up to the secondhand shop on my way to the university. I'd bung Alan a bit of cash and simply take his books back to my pad on King Street. This made things easier all round, except that I didn't want Alan to know I had all his old books – which meant I could no longer allow him to visit me at my bedsit.

Perhaps we didn't drive straight out to the Maiden Stone, we may have visited some stone circles first. It's hard to put everything back together in the correct order. I'd not had much sleep. I'd sat up most of the night before reading through some of Alan's old books. Thinking back through everything, we probably went to Archaeolink at Oyne first. I wanted a coffee on the way so Alan suggested we get cappuccinos in the Safeway café on the edge of Inverurie, quite close to the well-preserved Easter Aquhorthies stone circle. I thought a coffee would wake me up but I didn't want to go to a supermarket for my breakfast, so I made

Alan drive me out to Archaeolink. We didn't have to pay
the admission charge since we weren't there to see the
reconstructions of Iron-Age life. I got angry with Alan
since he insisted on seating Dudley at our table.

After Archaeolink we headed for the Maiden Stone. Alan
took a photograph of me standing in front of the easterly
side of the stone. I took a picture of him and Dudley from
the western side. Portraits done, we got back in the car
and drove to Esson's Car Park which abuts the Bennachie
Centre with its toilets and wide range of interpretative
material about the mountain. Personally, I don't understand
why this facility doesn't include a café. Anyway, we took the
steep and direct route to Mither Tap with Dudley strapped
to Alan's back. The first part of the ascent is a relatively
gentle forest walk and as we wended our way through the
pines, Alan discoursed on the relative merits of Grampian
Region as opposed to the Highlands proper. Aberdeenshire
had plenty of rich farmland, as well as mountains and forests.
Where it differed from the western side of Scotland was in its
relatively small number of lochs. While the sea was never far
away, the mountains didn't interact with water or rise sheer
from it in the spectacular fashion that made the Highlands
and Islands such a tourist trap.

The scenery of Grampian and the Hebrides present some
remarkable contrasts. Every observant traveller in the Western
Isles will readily acknowledge that the beauty of their
rugged shores is greatly enhanced by the sea and its sur-
roundings. In this aspect both Sutherland and the Hebrides
outdo even the peaks of Switzerland. Grand as are the
snow-clad peaks of the Alps, the absence of the ocean
in the land of John Calvin cannot fail to be regarded as
a serious want by anyone who has been accustomed to
watch the various aspects of that wondrous element. While
Aberdeenshire was blessed with the picturesque influence

of the sea on its eastern shore, it lacked the illimitable effect found in the west of Scotland where mountains rose sheer from the water. The sublime charm of the scenery of the Western Isles is founded on the three greatest powers in nature – the sky, the sea and the mountains.

The west of Scotland and the Hebrides had held pride of place in the imagination of the tourist and the bohemian since the roads to the isles had been opened up in the 18th century. Among the earliest published works to kindle this interest were Martin Martin's *Voyage To St Kilda* and *A Description of the Western Islands of Scotland*. The former was first published in 1697 and the latter in 1703. As Dudley explained to me while we gazed down at the countryside spread beneath us from the heights of Mither Tap, Martin has traditionally been credited with inspiring Boswell and Johnson to make their much-celebrated tour of Scotland. However, Dudley hastened to add, the influence of works such as Thomas Pennant's *A Tour Of Scotland in 1769* is often underestimated. Like Pennant, Boswell and Johnson visited Aberdeen but their recorded impressions of the town are supercilious indeed when contrasted with those of the Welshman who visited it four years before them.

'Aberdeen, a fine city, lying on a small bay formed by the Dee, deep enough for ships of two hundred tons. The town is about two miles in circumference, and contains thirteen thousand souls, and about three thousand in the suburbs; but the whole number of inhabitants between the bridges Dee and Don, which includes both the Aberdeens, and the interjacent houses, or hamlets, is estimated at twenty thousand. It once enjoyed a good share of the tobacco trade, but was at length forced to resign it to Glasgow, which was so much more conveniently situated for it. At present, its imports are from the Baltic, and a few merchants trade to the West Indies and North America. Its exports are stockings, thread, salmon, and oatmeal: the first is a most important article, as appears by the following state of it. For this manufacture, 20,800 pounds worth of wool is annually imported, and 1600 pounds worth of oil.

'Of this wool is annually made 69,333 pairs of stockings, worth, at an average, one pound and ten shillings per dozen. These are made by the country people, in almost all parts of this great county, who get four shillings per dozen for spinning and fourteen shillings per dozen for knitting; so that there is annually paid sixty-two thousand three hundred and twenty-nine pounds and fourteen shillings. And besides this there is about two thousand pounds value of stockings manufactured from the wool of the county, which encourages the breed of sheep much; for even as high as Invercauld, the farmer sells his sheep at twelve shillings apiece, and keeps them till they are four or five years old, for the sake of the wool. About two hundred combers are also employed constantly. Thread manufacture is another considerable article, tho' trifling in comparison of the woollen.'

While Johnson praised Pennant as the best traveller to Scotland he had ever read, in naming the journal he kept of his tour of 1773 *A Journey to the Western Islands of Scotland*, he helped set the fashion that has held steady from the romantics to modern-day hippies for favouring the Highlands over the more densely populated north-east coastal strip. Boswell, who accompanied Johnson on the jaunt, called his impressions of the trip *The Journal of a Tour to the Hebrides*. Once the sights of tourists bound for Scotland were fixed firmly to the west, travellers had little incentive to journey to the north-east. Both Sarah Murray, author of *A Companion and Useful Guide to the Beauties of Scotland*, and Dorothy Wordsworth, who compiled a journal entitled *Recollections of a Tour Made in Scotland A.D. 1803*, left Aberdeen off their itinerary. Johnson's approach was more caustic.

'To write of the cities of our own island with the solemnity of geographical description, as if we had been cast upon a newly discovered coast, has the appearance of very frivolous ostentation; yet as Scotland is little known to the greater part of those who may read those observations, it is not superfluous to relate that under the name of Aberdeen are comprised two towns, standing about a mile distant from each other, but governed, I think, by the same magistrates. Old Aberdeen is the ancient episcopal city in which are still to be seen the remains of the cathedral. It has the appearance of a town in decay, having been situated in times when commerce was yet unstudied, with very little attention to the commodities of the harbour. New Aberdeen has all the bustle of prosperous trade, and all the shew of increasing opulence. It is built by the waterside. The houses are large and lofty, and the streets spacious and clean. They build almost wholly with the granite used in the new pavement of the streets of London, which is well known not to want hardness, yet they shape it easily. It is beautiful and must be very lasting. What particular parts of commerce are chiefly exercised by the merchants of Aberdeen I have not inquired. The manufacture which forces itself up a stranger's eye is that of knit-stockings, on which the women of the lower class are visibly employed. In each of these towns there is a college, or in stricter language a university; for in both there are professors of the same parts of learning, and the colleges hold their sessions and confer degrees separately, with total independence of one on the other.'

Alan grew bored of ventriloquism and tossed the dummy to the ground. He pulled an apple from his rucksack and munched thoughtfully upon it as a young couple joined us on the peak. Once the 20-somethings decided they wanted to return to their car, Alan picked up the dummy and Dudley observed that Boswell and Johnson should be held personally responsible for the flood of romantics into the Highlands. Scott, Keats, Mendelssohn, Turner, Wordsworth, each was worse than those who'd proceeded them. Lowest of the lot, according to Dudley, was Lord Byron, who'd attended Aberdeen Grammar School. Dudley claimed William McGonagall's account of his trip to Balmoral was superior to all the crap written by professional romantics. There was only one other writer whose views on the Highlands Dudley valued and that was Bee Jay, a man who held the honour of being the missing link between McGonagall and the 'immortal' Bruce Chatwin. I have Alan's copies of Bee Jay's books before me as I write, signed first editions of *And It Came to Pass*, *The End of the Rainbow*, *Sunset on the Loch*, *Highland Pearls*, *Ardvreck's Shame* and *Scotland's Shangri-la*.

Before moving on, I should perhaps note that my first edition of *Scotland's Shangri-la* is not only signed, it still boasts a postal wrapper addressed in the author's hand to 'Mr H. Thorns, 5 The Grove, BISHOPTON, Renfrewshire'. The final two words are both underlined with 'Renfrewshire' ranged considerably below and to the right of 'BISHOPTON'. The wrapper is printed with the following information: '*Scotland's Shangri-la*. If undelivered return to S. Barker Johnson, Strath, Gairloch, Ross-shire.' Affixed to the letter are three stamps, two at three pence and one at seven and a half pence. All three stamps are franked and feature the head of Elizabeth II and the Scottish Lion Rampant. Inside are two letters from the author to Mr Thorns dated 29/11/67 and 24/10/72 respectively. Both letters are on headed stationery, the earlier bearing a stag's head, the latter the black outline of a stag on a mountainside. Both are hand-written in black ink and feature several

eccentric underlinings. The letter from 1972 even boasts
one particularly emphatic underlining in red felt pen.

I don't remember everything Dudley told me about Bee
Jay on that first climb up Mither Tap, but I do recall that
he disapproved of the author's comments about women
drivers and the hand motions allegedly made by Italians
when they are excited. Dudley's favourite Bee Jay book
was undoubtedly *The End of the Rainbow*. In this work the
author relates in unbelievable detail certain conversations he
had while courting his wife Fiona. Dudley was particularly
fond of the banter between Bee Jay and his future wife
during their first encounter on the Isle Of Mull. Bee Jay
explained that he was the author of a published book – being
careful not to describe it too accurately as self-published –
and that he was thinking of writing another tome. Fiona
replies: 'Oh how interesting.'

Dudley found Bee Jay's treatment of time in *The End of
the Rainbow* very curious, particularly in view of the fact
that inscribed in black ink beneath the author's signature
on the flyleaf of Alan's copy were the words: 'This is a
true story. S. B. J.' According to the narrative in *The End
of the Rainbow*, Stanley Barker Johnson or Bee Jay, began
courting his wife Fiona after he'd self-published *And It
Came to Pass* in 1962. *The End of the Rainbow* was self-
published in 1964 and yet the author confidently concludes
it with the observation: 'After a prolonged honeymoon in
Southern Ireland (including a visit to Blarney Castle, five
miles out of Cork, to kiss the magical Stone of Eloquence!)
we returned to the Dream House at Gairlock. As I have
said elsewhere, we have suffered no disillusionment; age
has not withered, nor have the years condemned our great
love.' Dudley therefore insisted that regardless of whether
Bee Jay was conscious of the fact or not, he was a proletarian
post-modernist since his unreliable first-person narration

was conclusive proof of the fact that he had no desire to constitute himself as a centred bourgeois subject. Several days later Alan repeated this observation virtually word for word while describing *Four Acres and a Donkey: The Memoirs of a Lavatory Attendant* by S. A. B. Rogers.

Having by this time read a good number of Alan's books, and thereby taken on much of his mind-set or subjectivity, I felt more than ready to counter Dudley's arguments. I suggested that rather than being a proletarian post-modernist, Bee Jay was actually a Bergsonian. Instead of treating time as homogenous, Bee Jay felt the intensity of his relationship with Fiona more than justified the claim that they'd been together for years, despite the fact that the period in question is unlikely to have exceeded twelve calendar months. Dudley wasted no time in denouncing the notion of durée as utterly irrelevant, insisting instead that Bee Jay was resorting to clichéd narrative conventions. Certainly, the sheer unbelievability of Bee Jay's prose made it more than likely that he was either completely deranged or else having fun at the expense of credulous readers.

Reading back over what I've written, it strikes me as more than probable that incredulous readers have long had a great deal of fun at Bee Jay's expense. Clearly much of the 'adulation' Christopher Isherwood received belonged to the hoary tradition of 'mock praise', and Bee Jay might easily be another instance of the same phenomenon. It is difficult to believe that Alan was being sincere when – after throwing Dudley limply to the ground – he insisted that *And It Came to Pass* was a classic, since in the introduction to this book Bee Jay makes it plain that he enjoyed a glass of Glenlivet. Although Alan was partial to a dram of Macallan, he certainly didn't like Glenlivet and was quite incapable of treating seriously any author who rated it as a whisky.

As far as I recall, the reason Alan carried Dudley up

Bennachie was to test the credibility of K. L. Callan's narrative in *69 Things to Do with a Dead Princess*. The author of this scurrilous text claimed that Princess Diana's death in Paris was faked and that she'd actually been strangled to death Thugee-style at Balmoral by an unknown assailant. The security services were extremely embarrassed about being caught short in this fashion and had handed the body over to K. L. Callan thinking he'd come up with an inventive means of disposing of it. Callan decided to take Diana around the Gordon District Stone Circle Trail as a means of luring tourists to the prehistoric delights of ancient Aberdeenshire. Of course, being a bit of a fanatic, he started off doing the Stone Circle Trail but ended by adding 58 places of interest to his original eleven-stop itinerary, hence the rather unfortunate title of his tome – *69 Things to Do with a Dead Princess*. Callan, of course, insisted he wasn't a necrophile but many of those who'd never read his scholarly text and knew it only by reputation unnaturally assumed that he was the last man to give the people's princess a proper seeing to. Alan wanted to test the feasibility of Callan's claims and so he'd weighted Dudley down with bricks and was attempting to repeat the heroic journey detailed in *69 Things to Do with a Dead Princess*.

After consulting Callan's peculiarly constructed narration and checking it against *The Stone Circle: Gordon's Early History*, I now realise that Alan reshuffled the order in which Callan made his pilgrimage to various ancient monuments and that even the author of *69 Things to Do with a Dead Princess* tended to wander off the trail that had been laid out for tourists. As far as my own narrative goes, what I've failed to mention is that between leaving Archaeolink and arriving at the Maiden Stone, we'd taken in the small symbol stones to be found in the grounds of Logie House. The day then proceeded pretty much as I've described it and this was in fact the first day Alan and I spent on the Stone Circle Trail, but the monuments we saw Callan visited on his second day of doing Gordon's ancient sites. For reasons best known to himself, Alan had decided to reverse the order of Callan's first two days with the corpse. Likewise, both Alan and Callan deviated from the instructions in the Stone Circle Trail booklet in deciding to take the steep rather than the gentle climb up Bennachie to Mither Tap.

Stone Circle Trail tourists are lured up Mither Tap to look at the Iron-Age hillfort just below the peak. Alan and I didn't bother with that. Alan laid me out on a flat rock at the peak and I had to pretend I was dead. He arranged my skirt around my waist and my knickers around my ankles. It was quite an effort to resist the urge to suck when Alan pushed his erect manhood into my open mouth. This was an experiment from which Alan hoped to discover what it was like to 69 a stiff, so I didn't chew despite an almost overwhelming temptation to do so. However, as Alan flicked his tongue over my clit I couldn't help writhing around a bit. Eventually I had an orgasm and pretty soon afterwards Alan shot a wad of his spunk into my mouth. We adjusted our clothing and Alan weighed Dudley down with the bricks that had come loose during his ventriloquist act. Once the dummy was strapped over the top of the rucksack on Alan's back, we made our way back to Esson's Car Park. I asked Alan what it was like getting a blow job from a corpse and he dismissed the query by saying it's a mighty peculiar sensation.

Having got back to the car and set off for new adventures, I began to think the Stone Circle Trail was a bit of a drag. We headed through Insch to the Dunnideer hillfort. Compared to Bennachie, Dunnideer is a tiny little hill. From the car park it only took us five minutes to get to the top, even with Dudley strapped to Alan's back. There were the ruins of a medieval castle as well as an Iron-Age fort at the summit. The remaining arch of the castle had looked better from the road as we'd approached it and the hillfort retained fewer of its stones than the one we'd just left at Mither Tap. After taking a few photographs, we made our way to the Picardy Stone a couple of miles to the north of Insch. Fortunately this Pictish stone wasn't a disappointment since it contained three symbols that were well delineated and easy to make out. Stupidly I didn't make any notes and I'm unable to remember what we saw carved into the stone.

I fell asleep in the car on the way back to Aberdeen. When Alan woke me I was still knackered. I'd not slept much the night before, so after a light meal at Owlies I went home alone. I hit the sack and although there was a lot of light streaming in through the curtains, it was only a matter of seconds before I was dreaming. Weary and sick, I arrived at some huts an hour's walk from Mither Tap. I realised these were the reconstructions of Iron-Age dwellings built as part of the Archaeolink complex, although the visitor centre they'd stood next to had disappeared. Dudley emerged from one of the huts carrying his genitals in his left hand. I lay on my back and Dudley lay on top of me. He put his prick in my hand. It was large and stiff. Letting the head pass through my fingers, I drew back the soft covering skin and I felt it bound in my hand.

Dudley shifted his weight. I felt his dick rub the moist lips of my cunt. It passed up me extending each humid fold and sensitive crease of my vagina. Then Dudley rammed home his prick with desperate energy and with a low moaning cry shot forth a torrent of hot spunk. I felt my cunt filled to overflowing. His molten genetics bubbling around my clit. Then I looked up and instead of Dudley I saw Alan. I closed my eyes and felt an orgasm wend its way through my body. When I opened my eyes I saw Dudley dressing in the thickening twilight. Once I'd adjusted my clothing we made our way into a hut where we came to a mutually beneficial agreement. I'd introduce Dudley to several of my sex-starved single friends if he'd help me kill Alan.

SIX

I WOKE early and made my way up Union Street to Union Grove. The rubbish was being collected that morning and so the streets were lined with bin bags. As is their wont, the local sea gulls had broken into the sacks awaiting collection in the hope of finding tasty morsels. As a result, the streets were strewn with litter. Alan's car was parked outside his tenement and Dudley was sitting up on the back seat. I hoped he hadn't been left out overnight without so much as a blanket thrown over him. Books were spilling from a rubbish bag close to Alan's car. I clocked various titles by Christopher Burns – *About the Body*, *The Flint Bed*, *The Condition of Ice*. I shoved the books back into the bag and placed the sack at the bottom of the stairwell that led up to Alan's flat.

I got Alan out of bed and chided him for throwing out books as if they were just rubbish. He insisted Christopher Burns was rubbish, as were all the other literary – and Alan stressed literary – failures he'd treated as refuse. After a few minutes of verbal ping-pong Alan dressed. As we left the flat he picked up the bag of books I'd dragged into the stairwell. I made Alan drop them and as he did so the Christopher Burns paperbacks fell to the floor. I retrieved the spillage and said I'd collect the rest of my swag later. Alan told me that the Old Aberdeen Bookshop wouldn't buy works of this type. I said they'd be welcomed by Oxfam or Cancer

Care. Alan sneered that you couldn't even give away these forgotten men – and he said men, not men and women – of literature. He pointed at the strapline on the cover of *The Flint Bed*: 'Shortlisted for the Whitbread Novel of the Year 1989'. Burns was one of the reforgotten. He got close but never broke through, it was his misfortune to be more talented than the likes of Ivy Compton-Burnett.

We got into the car and headed for Inverurie. I flicked through *About the Body*, came across a story that featured an Elvis Presley imitator. Alan dismissed Burns' prose as mannered. As too self-conscious to appeal to anyone who understood trash. Unfortunately he was right. We discussed the way in which the labour of unsuccessful writers, artists and musicians valorises the best-selling efforts of those who succeed. Burns had negotiated his way through to publication and respectful literary reviews. But having opted for the literary genre, there was no way his books could really rock. He wasn't going to pick up a hard-core following or sell over the long term like Guy Debord and William Burroughs. He had no devoted readership and little chance of remaining in print for long, let alone being republished in 30 or 40 years' time. In short a typical mid-list author.

We drove through Dyce and past the airport. Alan wanted to practise his ventriloquism, so it was Dudley who pointed out Tyrebagger Hill from the back seat. I'd almost forgotten about the oral sex we'd had at the recumbent stone circle up there a few days before but it came back with the clarity of a recurring dream. Dudley was talking about the writer Duncan McLean, describing him as almost a local lad, what with being born in Fraserburgh and growing up in some wee village outside Banchory. Dudley informed me that McLean's first book *Bucket of Tongues* featured a story entitled 'The Druids Shite It, Fail To Show', in which a bunch of middle-class soccer casuals get pissed at a fictional location loosely based on the Tyrebagger stanes. I asked Dudley how he knew the hooligans were middle-class. He told me that was easy. Everyone knew that the Aberdeen supporters who'd minced their way to tabloid notoriety back in the 80s were a bunch of bourgeois tossers. Their badly-dressed mascot Jay Allan even boasted about this in his illiterate attempt at autobiography *Bloody Casuals: Diary of a Football Hooligan*.[7]

Dudley described McLean as a proletarian post-modernist who wanted to give Dyce the psychogeographical treatment, exaggerating the distance from the heliport and the nearest bus stop. Making out that a bunch of wankers from the village were going out of their way and up more than one hill to get to what was actually an easily accessible local landmark. It went without saying that it was the intellectual shortcomings of the characters – a pig-ignorant bunch of bourgeois fantasists – that led them to believe that the Tyrebagger stanes were erected by Druids. The publishers of the book wouldn't know truth from fiction in terms of either setting or milieu, but locals reading the story would have a good laugh at the media clowns down in Edinburgh and London being taken in by this baloney!

Alan interrupted Dudley by going into an old-time barker's rant he often used when interacting with the dummy. I don't remember exactly what he used to say but the gist of it is this: 'On top of Tyrebagger Hill there is a heathen temple. It consists of ten long stones placed in a circular form; the diameter of it is about twenty four feet. The highest of the stones, which stand on the south side, are about nine feet above ground; the lowest, which are on the north side, four and a half. There is one stone placed on its edge, betwixt the two southmost stones which is about six feet high. They are all rough stones and of great bulk. Likewise, scattered throughout north-east Scotland there are to be seen many very great stones, brought together, and set on end; some one way; and some another; and, for the most part, on tops or risings of hills. It is the common tradition that they have been the places of pagan sacrifices; for it is like that it hath been a ceremony of the heathen worship to be on high places. I never minded to observe if there could be any footsteps of fire perceived on these stones. We find Jacob set up a stone and if this have been a ceremony of religion in these days, as is like, the pagan idolatry, no doubt, has had something in imitation thereof.'

Once Alan had done his party piece, Dudley said he'd read a lot of Duncan McLean's work, *Blackden* for example, which was set out Banchory way. There McLean cocked a snook at self-styled metropolitan sophisticates by unfavourably comparing the Bogie and the Gadie – at the back o' Bennachie – to an American river he claimed was called the Cranberry. That gave Dudley a few belly laughs at the expense of McLean's literary puffers who'd promoted his prose as merciless realism! Alongside McLean, the other local author the dummy really rated was a retired primary school teacher called Doris Davidson. This Aberdeen-based writer had penned a number of romantic classics including *The Brow of the Gallowgate*, *The Road to Towanbrae*, *Time Shall Reap* and *Waters of the Heart*. While McLean ironically confronted the concerns of what the media configured as young males, Davidson addressed the fantasies of those who allowed themselves to be constructed as middle-aged women. Constant references to 'rearing beasts' drummed home Davidson's much repeated message that men simply couldn't control their sexual urges.

Dudley's discourse on Davidson's historical romances was interrupted by our arrival at Safeway on the outskirts of Inverurie. Alan carried Dudley into the supermarket café and propped him up on a chair while I ordered two breakfasts. Being relatively early in the morning, there weren't many customers in the supermarket and I was quite surprised by the pleasant ambience of the Safeway café. Large plate-glass windows meant there was plenty of natural light and even though the view onto the customer car park wasn't exactly scenic, it was pleasant. As we ate Alan quipped that I had some rare treats in store as I worked my way through his bin bag of literary junk. He ran through some names. The majority I didn't recognise but I knew Robert McCrum because at the time he was literary editor at *The Observer*.

McCrum's weekly column had often irritated me and I stopped reading it towards the end of 1998. The final straw was a piece in which McCrum suggested that over the past few years there'd been resistance to business forces entering the book market. McCrum's time scale was several centuries out and I could only conclude that he didn't know about the crucial role the book played in the development of capitalism. In many ways the book can be considered the first commodity and whole books had been written about the perfection of this commodity form. I figured that if McCrum didn't know his arse from his elbow then, alongside virtually every other newspaper columnist employed on 'Fleet Street', he really wasn't worth reading. I wish to stress that I am not trying to suggest McCrum suffers from an inability to do his job. *The Observer*, like a great many other papers, chooses to fill its pages with columns and a crucial qualification for landing one of these regular spots appears to be a propensity towards emotional self-indulgence and a refusal to do research. Columnists are expected to fill columns with words and judged on such criteria McCrum remains a consummate professional.

Alan was delighted that I recognised McCrum's name and between shovelling forkfuls of fry-up into his gob, he whooped out a hundred and one put-downs of the would-be author. According to Alan, McCrum was a time-server and this was patently evident from his first book *In the Secret State*. Nominally a thriller, the work is really about office politics and how one gets ahead in a bureaucracy. Typically, Alan observed, McCrum mistook position for power and singularly failed to understand that bureaucrats are simply acting out a script. For someone to exercise power they must necessarily be in a position to effect change. A literary editor or spook who merely acts out the decision-making process in ritual form, reproducing already established patterns of behaviour, has very little real power. McCrum was Alan's best example. When McCrum had been a literary editor at Faber and Faber he'd patently failed to break the mould of what had been published before he got there. Of course, given McCrum's connections, he was able to get his books published and favourably reviewed, but he could not be described as influential. He was every inch the bureaucrat and would never be an opinion shaper.

Alan was still talking about McCrum's first book as he bundled Dudley into the car and we made our way to the Brandsbutt symbol stone. This was located in a housing estate very close to Safeway. At one time there had been a stone circle abutting the Brandsbutt stone but that had been destroyed long ago. Dudley was wheeled out of the car and we took a few photos. I thought Alan might move on to the subject of Kevin Callan's *69 Things to Do with a Dead Princess*, but he had yet to exhaust the subject of Robert McCrum. As we got into the car Alan made a series of jokes about the Byron complex that McCrum was alleged to suffer from. Of course, like Byron, the hero of *In the Secret State* has a limp but Alan cackled, the thing that really hobbled in this novel was the prose.

At this point we were neither following Callan's route

nor that of the Stone Circle Trail. Alan was chuckling about the many clangers in McCrum's first book. Specifically he was in hysterics about the fact that McCrum quite earnestly used a character's rereading of Carlyle as evidence that this stereotype loved history, blissfully unaware that no one who knew the first thing about the subject would treat the author of *The French Revolution* and *History of Frederick the Great* as a serious historian, particularly when it was the flaws in the latter work that made it one of Hitler's favourite books. Once we'd reached the village of Daviot, Alan pulled up in a car park by a scout hut. A short walk through some trees brought us to Loanhead of Daviot stone circle. Immediately in front of us was a recumbent stone with two flankers and eight others making up the circle with a kerbed ring cairn inside. Just to the east was an enclosed Bronze-Age cremation cemetery. All of this was set on a gentle slope with the countryside to the north spread out before us.

Alan threw Dudley down on the recumbent stone and the dummy announced languidly that he was tired and wished Alan and me to dance and play before him. We waltzed around the stone circle and simultaneously removed our clothes. Alan pushed his legs between my thighs and in this way our genitals and bottoms were paraded before Dudley in the lewdest possible fashion. As we went on we grew more excited, smacking each other's rumps until Alan grew bold enough to pull some hairs out of my cunt. Then he kissed my sex better, licked it copiously and before long we were fucking.

The ground was rough. Alan got up and dislodging Dudley from his resting place, reclined on the recumbent stone. I bent over Alan, petting his prick and smiling as it stood up stiffly. It was about this time that I spotted two girls of my age watching us from the edge of the wood. I winked at them as I drew down the soft foreskin and uncovered Alan's large swelling head, red and shining like a ripe plum. Alan, who had also spotted our two admirers, directed me to sit on his face and called the girls over saying he'd like them to play with his prick and arse. I clambered onto the recumbent stone and knelt with my knees on each side of Alan's shoulders so that I could place my cunt full on his mouth. One of the girls lay between Alan's legs and lifting them up, pressed back his hams and thus gained access to his upturned *derrière*, into which she thrust her wet tongue as far as she could. The other held Alan's prick in her mouth but without frigging it, which, I observed, she carefully avoided as she sucked the head and gently stirred the balls.

We carried on in this way for quite some time, the sun beating down upon us, until Alan and I had simultaneous orgasms. The two girls had yet to come, so Alan and I jumped down from the recumbent and they leant back against it as we hitched up their skirts, pulled down their knickers and got to work with our tongues. Once our new friends had enjoyed orgasms, we all adjusted our clothing and got into the car. We dropped the girls in Inverurie, then made our way back past Safeway to the Easter Aquhorthies stone circle. Fortunately the route was signposted since we had to make our way up a single-track road for the best part of a mile. There was an old 2CV occupying one of the spaces in the minuscule Easter Aquhorthies car park when we arrived. We hauled Dudley out of the back seat and made our way up a track, forked right and quickly found ourselves at the stanes. I've forgotten what Alan told me about McCrum's second novel *A Loss of Heart* as we walked back to the circle.

A 40-something hippie mama was doing a lap of the circle, placing her hands on each stone, closing her eyes and hoping to feel the energies. A considerably straighter-looking man was attempting to keep two children entertained. As soon as the bairns clocked Dudley they wanted to play with the dummy. Alan did a bit of ventriloquism, getting Dudley to explain that he liked to slit the throats of youngsters and fry up their kidneys. The kids were enthralled, their father was grateful to get a break and their mother was so consumed by her quest for mystic energies that she ignored patter that in different circumstances she may have considered offensive.

Taking his leave from the dysfunctional family, Alan returned to the subject of Robert McCrum. He began talking about the literary time-server's third novel *The Fabulous Englishman*. Alan tittered that in this work McCrum's literary powers extended no further than describing an Austrian train station as typically Austrian and the air on a station platform as carrying the smells of a train station. When Alan told me this I thought he was exaggerating McCrum's hack style. However, when I eventually tracked down a paperback copy of the novel I found these extremely literal descriptions on pages 66 and 67 exactly as Alan had assured me I would. Mercifully, McCrum avoided the accusation that he did not know his material by making his main character a failed novelist. As we bypassed Inverurie town centre, Alan observed that being a dedicated bureaucrat McCrum not only succeeded in getting this novel published, he even received puffs in the press for his brilliant descriptions. I wondered why McCrum bothered, since most of those who read the book must have done so for the cheap laughs to be had at his expense. It was the McGonagall syndrome all over again.

By the time we reached the Aberdeen side of Inverurie, Alan had exhausted Robert McCrum's prose as an object of ridicule. He was kept busy justifying his deviation from the route described by K. L. Callan in *69 Things to Do with a Dead Princess*. Alan claimed that we'd needed a decent breakfast and having headed out to the Safeway café it had made sense to re-order the first day of the journey described in Callan's book. Alan's reasoning was that we were merely attempting to test the credibility of Callan's claims by carting a dummy weighted with bricks around the Gordon District Stone Circle Trail, we weren't trying to recreate the journey Callan described.

Broomend of Crichie doesn't look like much now but a few thousand years ago it was probably the most important ritual centre in what subsequently became known as north-east Scotland. We swung left by a petrol station and parked the car behind it. We climbed over a gate and across an overgrown field. I couldn't see the stones but Alan led me straight to them. I didn't clock the ditched henge in the field until we got right up to it. Long grass covered the dip and the weed growth was even more luxuriant around the remains of the stone circle. Only two of the original stones remained and they'd been disturbed. A Pictish symbol stone had been moved from its original position 150 yards away and placed alongside these stanes when a 19th-century railway line was being laid. There were entrances to the henge from the north and south and lines of standing stones had once led from these to other circles long since destroyed.

Alan plonked Dudley down beside the symbol stone and took a photograph of the dummy. Then he picked me up and pulled me against him while simultaneously steadying himself against one of the other stones. Alan forced one of his knees between my legs and lifting my skirt proceeded to yank down my panties. I leant back against Alan and spread my legs so that he could rub my clit. Soon he was working one of his fingers in and out of my moist chink. I pushed myself upwards and worked my hands behind my back. I fumbled for a few seconds but before long I'd undone my partner's belt, unzipped his flies and pushed his pants down around his ankles. Alan removed his finger from my hole and I guided his prick up the moist passage. I had Alan pressed back against the stone and worked his meat at my own pace. Alan was caught between a rock and a hard place. When he came it was because I wanted him to shoot his hot spunk into my steaming cunt. We had a simultaneous orgasm and afterwards, while I was still speared on Alan's semi-flaccid dick, he used his ventriloquist's skills to transform Dudley into a voyeur who thanked us profusely for fulfilling his deepest fantasy.

After adjusting our clothing we got back into the car and headed down the A96 to Kintore. We parked in the centre of the village, right by the kirkyard. I stood with one arm around Dudley as I leant against the side of the symbol stone in Kintore churchyard while Alan took a snapshot. Alan carried Dudley around to the other side of the stone, where he handed me the camera so that I could take a picture of the two of them holding hands. After this we got back in the car and made our way to the standing stones near the west gate of Dunecht House. These stanes provided a backdrop for more photographs. At some point before we parked the car to one side of Midmar Kirk, Alan began talking about Nicholas Royle. I recognised the name as that of an anthologist and critic. Alan said he couldn't fault my knowledge as far as it went but that Royle's other skills had clearly been honed by his extensive output of fiction. In many ways Royle was working a similar territory to Conrad Williams, making good use of an intimate knowledge of both literary and genre fiction. Alan certainly rated Royle's first novel *Counterparts*, which boasted a schizophrenic narration that could only be read as a full-frontal assault on the bourgeois subject.

Midmar was unlike any of the stone circles I'd seen so far, not only was it situated next to a church but a graveyard had been built around it. A very well-maintained lawn was laid out inside the circle of stones and the resultant over-definition made me think of it as a hyperrealist recreation of an ancient monument. The fact that the recumbent and its two flankers were massive added to the impression that Midmar was nothing other than an overblown simu-lation. Finally, the grading of the stones was simply wrong, indicating that at some point they'd been disturbed and whoever had restored them had done so incorrectly. Once we'd placed ourselves on the lawn inside this circle, my companions began babbling about assorted Aberdeenshire antiquities. I don't remember exactly what Dudley said but the gist of it may be gained from some automatic writing I recently made after shoving a vibrator into my cunt as a means of opening my body up to psychic influences and subtle messages.

'The worship of rude stones, as representing or containing a deity is supposed to have come from the fall of meteoric showers, which the ancients naturally regarded with deep wonder, and imagined to be representatives sent down from heaven to man. Of the continuity of religious worship at these dedicated spots, through all the developments of paganism and through the most absurd development of all, from paganism to Christianity, there cannot really be any valid doubt. If the outlying stone is due SW, and if the normal line from the centre of the recumbent stone is due north-east, the magician looking along that line will see the sun rise at midsummer, whether he stands at the outlying stone or at the middle of the recumbent stone. The circles were clocks and the magician had his way of making his announcements of the passage of time by night without making any noise or waking any one of his community, he simply burnt a handful of dry grass. Likewise, the Gaelic *clachan* (church) means "stones". Kirk was so called because it was the one stone building in the neighbourhood. But local enquiries show that in many parts the question "are you going to kirk?" is put in the term "are you going to the stones?"'

Of course, modern research suggests that the chief alignments of recumbent stone circles are lunar rather than solar, and Alan was not slow to highlight other peculiarities in Dudley's pronouncements. After trashing the views expressed by his dummy, Alan pointed out the Sunhoney stone circle on farmland about a mile away. Rather than offering clues to the identity of the lost tribe, a number of seekers had concluded that this site was the scene of macabre occult practices. On 3 June 1944 John Foster Forbes took his scryer Miss Iris Campbell to the monument to make a psychometric reading, the results of this bizarre session are recorded in the former's *Giants of Britain*, a masterpiece of crank research. Forbes and Campbell are not the only nutters to conclude these eldritch stones mutely signal some unspeakable evil. Hippie headcase Paul Screeton in the book *Quicksilver Heritage* claimed that black magic has been practised at the site in recent years and found the circle so unpleasant that he says in print he would not like to revisit it.

When Alan told me this I knew instinctively where everything we were doing together would end. After we'd taken some pictures of Dudley sprawled on the lawn enclosed by the Midmar stone circle, Alan suggested we make our way to Sunhoney. I insisted we wait, we were not ready, for the time being we should stick to the trail K. L. Callan had laid out for us in *69 Things to Do with a Dead Princess*. Cullerlie was our next destination, some low-lying stanes set amid rich farmland and built without a recumbent. The circle contained a number of tiny ring cairns. Alan leant Dudley against one of the eight stones that constituted the main attraction and took a photograph. After checking his watch Alan said we had to split. We headed back to Aberdeen along the A944. When we pulled up in Union Grove my friend Rita was walking away from Alan's flat. My companion leapt out of his car and went chasing after her. I ducked into the stairwell to retrieve the books I'd left there but they'd gone. By the time I got back onto the street, Rita was touching Alan's arse as he locked his car. I told Alan I'd see him in the morning and went home. I was more than happy about the fact that Rita had shown up so unexpectedly, I wanted some time on my own to read Christopher Burns and a whole bunch of other things.

SEVEN

I DREAMT I stood on the summit of a precipice, whose downward height no eye could measure, but for the fearful waves of a fiery ocean that lashed, and blazed, and roared at its bottom, sending its burning spray far up, so as to drench my dreaming self in sulphurous rain. The whole glowing ocean below was alive – every billow bore an agonising soul that rose like a wreck or a putrid curse on the waves of earth's ocean – uttered a shriek as it burst against that adamantine precipice – sank – and rose again to repeat the tremendous experiment! Every billow of fire was thus instinct with immortal and agonising existence – each was freighted with a soul that rose on the burning wave in torturing hope, burst on the rock in despair, added its eternal shriek to the roar of that fiery ocean, and sunk to rise again – in vain – and forever!

Suddenly I felt myself flung half-way down the precipice. I stood, in my dream, tottering on a crag midway down the precipice – I looked upwards, but the upper air showed only blackness unshadowed and impenetrable – but, blacker than that blackness, I could distinguish the giant outstretched arm of Dudley that held me as in sport on the ridge of that infernal precipice, while another, that seemed in its motions to hold fearful and invisible conjunction with the arm that grasped me, as if both belonged not to Dudley but some being too vast and horrible even for the imagery of a dream to shape, pointed upwards to a dial-plate fixed on the top of that precipice, and which the flashes of that ocean made fearfully conspicuous. I saw Dudley's mysterious single hand revolve – I saw it reach the appointed number of 69 – I shrieked in my dream, and, with that strong impulse often felt in sleep, burst from the arm that held me, to arrest the motion of the hand.

In the effort I fell and, falling, grasped at aught that might save me. My fall seemed perpendicular – there was nothing to save me – the rock was smooth as ice – the ocean of fire broke at its foot! Suddenly a group of figures appeared, ascending as I fell. I grasped at them successively – first Dudley, then Alan – Rita – Jill – Karen – Hannah – Suzy – Michael – all passed me – to each I seemed in my slumber to cling in order to break my fall – all ascended the precipice. I caught at each in my downward flight, but all forsook me and ascended.

My last despairing reverted glance was fixed on the dial of sexual variations – the upraised black arm seemed to push forward the hand – 0 then 1 then 69 – it was stuck fast at the oral fixation stage – I was a baby – I fell – I sank – I blazed – I shrieked! The burning waves boomed over my sinking head, and the dial of sexual variations boomed out my dreadful secrets – 'Anna had sex with a ventriloquist's dummy!' – and the waves of the burning ocean answered, as they lashed the adamantine rock – 'Anna's desires are an ocean, an illusion, and now she will make love to herself, to me, the sea!'[8] At this, I awoke. The entry bell was ringing. It was Karen, one of my friends from college. I buzzed her in to the tenement.

It was raining and the streets were not yet busy. I put the door on the latch. Moments later Karen pushed her way into my bedsit and handed me a curt note from one of my professors. I threw it into the bin. He wanted me to provide an explanation of why I'd missed a tutorial. I decided to lie and say I was sick. A terrible fever. I'd been laid up in bed for days. Karen made tea as I dressed. She poured me a cup and we exchanged pleasantries. She was concerned about me, said she couldn't cover up my absences from college much longer. I told her I'd go in soon, but insisted I should stay off sick for one more day. I scribbled a note for her to hand in on my behalf. Karen giggled at her complicity in my skiving. I made toast and shared it with my friend.

The rain eased off as I made my way up Union Street to Union Grove. I let myself into Alan's flat. I don't remember exactly when he gave me the key but I know it was some time before I had the dream about the burning sea. Alan was in bed, asleep with Rita. When I woke them Alan wanted a three-way fuck but I said later. We had things to do and bed-hopping could wait until it was dark. Alan resigned himself to waiting for nookie and got up. Rita wanted to waste time putting on make-up but I told her not to bother since we'd be climbing Tap o' Noth later and she'd only sweat it off. Alan was out of both coffee and eggs, so we just jumped into his car and headed for Inverurie. I wanted to go to a café in the town centre but Alan thought it unlikely that any of them did anything but instant coffee, so we went to Safeway instead.

Rita was embarrassed when we propped Dudley up in a chair at our table. The women doling out the fry-ups recognised us from the day before and were friendly. I used the toilets, which were spotlessly clean. We drove through Oyne, Insch and Kennethmont to get to Rhynie. Our first stop was the Old Kirkyard. This was a disappointment. The Pictish symbol stones had been moved into a horrid wooden construction to protect and preserve them from moss damage. The effect wasn't hypperreal, it was mundane. There was no longer any aura of mystery about the stones.

We spent a couple of minutes looking at them and left. There were more symbol stones on Rhynie Square, a very pleasant tree-lined village green. The atmosphere was picturesque rather than sublime and above all else pleasing. We lingered among these stones because one goes to such sites for the atmosphere as much as anything else.

Scurdargue car park at the bottom of Tap o' Noth was only a few minutes' drive from Rhynie. Alan weighed Dudley down with some bricks and slung the dummy over his back. We had to explain to Rita that we were attempting to test the credibility of novelist K. L. Callan's non-fiction work *69 Things to Do with a Dead Princess*. Rita found it hard to believe that anyone would even claim to have carted the corpse of a dead princess around the principal monuments of Aberdeenshire, let alone actually do it. Fortunately Alan had a copy of Callan's tract in the car, so I was able to flash it at her. While I was doing this I clocked a bunch of film books Alan had stacked behind the driver's seat. I figured he was intending to sell them to the Old Aberdeen Bookshop. I made a mental note to ask him about them before we headed back to the Granite City.

We cut across a tree-fringed field. Then along a hedge-lined path and across another field. From there a path wound around the hill which was oval and extremely regular in shape. Alan complained that the ascent was boring. He preferred roughness and sudden variation. The local tourist board went to great lengths to stress that the hill was composed of Rhynie Chert, a rock that contains some of the oldest known fossils in the world, including that of *Rhyniella praecursor*, the earliest insect fossil. While this might have provided fuel for the imagination of a horror writer such as H. P. Lovecraft, it didn't do much for Alan because the fossils were microscopic. Alan set a cracking pace despite having Dudley and a bunch of bricks strapped to his back. Rita whinged that the climb up the hill, which took all of 40 minutes, was exhausting.

Our collective mood improved when we reached the vitrified hillfort that topped Tap o' Noth. The views were spectacular and the Iron-Age stoneworks impressive. Having carried the dummy weighted with bricks up the hill, Alan quipped that he wouldn't have wanted the responsibility of getting the thousands of boulders that constituted the fort to the top. The stones were ranged in an oval around the flat top of the hill, forming a defensive wall. Once the rocks had been put in place, brushwood was heaped over them and set alight to create the vitrification. Heated, they'd melted together to form an impregnable fortress. We walked around the wall of stones. The fortifications were even more impressive than those at Mither Tap. It was a great pity Tap o' Noth's regular features rendered it less impressive as a mountain.

I'd studied the Stone Circle Trail booklet and as we stood taking in the view commented that we'd completed our itinerary. Alan laughed and said there were hidden features not included in the pamphlet, such as White Hill recumbent stone circle. When I asked Alan how he knew this he told me to check the notice board in the car park at the bottom of the hill. He'd glanced at it on the way up and spotted this extra attraction. Besides, my companion chuckled, White Hill is mentioned in *69 Things to Do with a Dead Princess*, so I'd obviously not been doing my research very thoroughly. Rita, who was thumbing though Callan's book, commented that having got the dummy up Tap o' Noth we'd proved that it was possible to get a corpse to all the locations mentioned in this text. She then suggested that having done this, there was no point in taking Dudley to any of the other sites. In response, both Alan and I insisted that he'd definitely be going with us when we visited Sunhoney.

Once we were sitting down on the edge of the fort, with a can of pop passing between us, I asked Alan about the film books in his car. As I'd surmised, he was planning to sell them. Alan explained that he'd not seen many of the Japanese sex movies described by Jack Hunter in *Eros in Hell: Sex, Blood & Madness in Japanese Cinema*, but some of the other tomes very accurately described his teenage cinema viewing in London. Alan had enjoyed reading *Meat Is Murder: An Illustrated Guide to Cannibal Culture* by Mikita Brottman, since he'd been a huge fan of movies like *Cannibal Holocaust* and *The Texas Chainsaw Massacre* when he'd been a kid. He lamented the steady loss of cinemas with the advent of video. He'd frequented flea pits all over London when he was young and now most of them had disappeared. The eminently social activity of going to the pictures had been replaced by the private vice of watching videos. The two things had very little in common. Alan insisted that he was unable to constitute himself as a bourgeois subject thanks, at least in part, to the influence of proletarian post-modernism in the form of horror films that lacked centred subjects.

While Bev Zalcock utilised certain strands of feminist theory in defence of trash film in *Renegade Sisters: Girl Gangs on Film*, Alan preferred Carol J. Clover's unashamedly 'high-brow' exploration of 'low-brow' culture in *Men, Women and Chainsaws: Gender in the Modern Horror Film*. For Alan, everything that was contradictory in Clover's approach constituted her most productive critical contributions. He particularly appreciated Clover's extended commentary on the flaws inherent in the notion of the 'male gaze', despite the fact that her arguments were still hopelessly enmeshed in the utterly discredited discourse of Freudian psychology. How anyone could believe in the unconscious was completely beyond Alan's understanding. As far as he was concerned, superstitions of this type differed very little from traditional religion.

Alan seemed to pass into a trance while describing in excessive detail the cinemas at which he'd first seen various trash films, so Rita and I put our arms around one another. As we petted I became quite excited and after Rita thrust a finger up my hole, I realised it was dripping wet. To excite Rita I drew up my things and poked my bottom out, hoping that she might suck and kiss it. My friend told me excitedly that my arse was splendid with its great fat cheeks bulging out on either side, and a most delicious randy-looking cunt gaping in the hollow between. Rita pulled open my lips with her fingers to view the rich carmine of my interior folds all glistening with the dew of love. Then drawing up her own dress in a bid to attract Alan's attention, she knelt before me and plunged her face between my wide-spread thighs, and kissed my cunt with such vehemence that I let out a loud moan of pleasure. This noise was enough to rouse Alan from his dreams and so Rita ate me out while our companion dropped his trousers and proceeded to work her hole with his throbbing manhood. After much grunting and groaning and many cries of pleasure, constituting a good 20 minutes' worth of fucking, all three of us came together in an ego-negating simultaneous orgasm.

After this orgy of lust we sat for some time contemplating the play of sunlight on the land spread beneath us. We descended Tap o' Noth in a buzz of conversation, which flitted from movies to records and books. I don't remember everything that was said but at one point Alan was gushing in his praise of *Confessions of a Dangerous Mind: An Unauthorized Autobiography* by Chuck Barris. This, Alan said, was a celebrity book with a difference. The tedious detailing of the Barris career from nonentity to the crowning glory of the *The Gong Show* was, of course, pretty much what you'd expect in a work of this kind. But rather than inducing passivity among his readership, Barris had constructed the book dialectically and in this fashion encouraged a critical attitude towards show-biz tittle-tattle. To do this Barris ran the narrative of his public career against a counter-narrative about his 'secret' work as a CIA assassin. Rather than offering verities for the faithful, Barris wanted people to question the veracity of everything he stood for. According to Alan, a similar device was used to even greater effect in *Bad Wisdom* by Bill Drummond and Mark Manning, where each of the writers offered a contradictory account of the same event.

With this discussion still ringing in my ears we drove back through Kennethmont and Insch to Bennachie. I'd wanted to go to White Hill but Alan insisted that we had other business that needed attending to first. Rita didn't seem to care where we went, she knew even less than I did about the stanes and was happy simply going along for the ride. Our first stop was Druidstone. Alan parked his Fiesta just off the road, weighed Dudley down with a few bricks and took off through a field. There were two guys with a dog, guns and a pick-up truck at the back of the field. They were loading up game they'd just shot and Alan fell into conversation with them. They weren't sportsmen, they were local and intended to eat the birds they'd killed. When Alan said we were on our way to the Druidstone they nodded knowingly and gave detailed directions on where to find it.

Druidstone is part of a ruined Bronze-Age circle. We had to trudge through a field of wind-damaged wheat before we found it at the bottom of a slope close to some derelict buildings. Bennachie looked beautiful as it brooded above us. I know brooded sounds as if it should be used with 'sublime' rather than 'beautiful' but I'm deliberately mixing my metaphors to express the contradictory emotions the mountain conjures up. Alan dumped Dudley by a stone at the edge of the ruined circle and when Rita cradled the dummy in her arms I felt jealous. Once Alan had taken four pictures of my friend canoodling the dummy, I insisted he take a photo of Dudley with his hand underneath my skirt.

After returning to the car our next stop was Cothiemuir Wood. This recumbent circle wasn't visible from the road but the men we'd met near Druidstone had said the path to the stanes was barred with a wooden pole and that opposite it there was an avenue of trees. I spotted a stone from the circle through some trees as we ambled along. This was a perfect way of coming upon a circle. First catching a glimpse from a distance and gradually getting to see more as we approached it. Cothiemuir Wood, within the grounds of Castle Forbes, seems originally to have consisted of eleven upright stones, mostly about seven feet high, forming a circle 25 yards in diameter. The two flankers were nine and a half feet high, and 15 feet asunder, the space between them being occupied by a massive recumbent stone upwards of five feet in diameter and thirteen and a half feet in length, lying on the west side of the circle. In the middle of the circle was a quantity of loose stones and near the centre, a slab of four or five feet square, covering a small pit open on the south side. The recumbent with its two flankers plus two uprights was still correctly positioned. The three other uprights that still stood were no longer vertical and these leaning stanes spoke of the ravages of time. At Cothiemuir Wood I took my skirt off and pulled my knickers down around my ankles, allowing Alan to take a picture of Dudley entangled in my arms.

Motoring on, we saw the remains of Old Keig stone circle from the road as we approached it. However, the monument had disappeared by the time we parked at the far end of the avenue of trees in which it was located. We had to clamber over barbed wire to gain access to the avenue and rather than strapping Dudley to his back from the onset, Alan passed the dummy across this obstacle to me. At first our passage was blocked by recently planted saplings but once we got past these into the older trees the going was a little easier. Nevertheless, the path we picked up was quite overgrown and I rather wished I'd geared up in jeans since the brambles tore at my tights. The circle came back into view once we were up close to it. The monument, which was blemished by a great many more imperfections than Cothiemuir Wood, would have been 66 feet in diameter before its ruination. In the circumference of the circle there were two upright stones, the flankers, nine feet above ground, with the recumbent being about 16 feet long, six feet high and five feet broad at one end, of a quadrangular form and placed on the south side of the circle. Rita got her tits out before allowing Alan to take a photograph of Dudley embracing her.

On the way back to Aberdeen Alan parked on a back road running off the A96. We walked past the ruins of Balquhain Castle, a large farmhouse and several cottages before cutting into a field of rape. The monument we sought was in the next field. Balquhain stone circle had suffered only slightly less damage than Old Keig, the recumbent and three uprights were still in position, the rest being scattered about nearby. Just a few feet from the circle was a quartz outlying stone and close up it was truly dazzling. Likewise, the view of Mither Tap from Balquhain was superb. All things considered, however, this circle was more impressive when viewed from the A96. At a distance the grass growing around the smashed-up stones stood out as a green circle in a sea of rape, giving the monument much-needed definition. Close up, this effect was lost and the stones were a disappointingly jumbled mess. Rita and I made a truce, so that when Alan took Dudley's picture I sat on his plastic face with my skirt around my waist, while my companion simulated giving the dummy a blow job by positioning her head between his legs. After this Alan pointed out some cup marks on one of the stones. Rita asked me the time and then told Alan to stop fucking about. She needed to get back to Aberdeen because she'd promised to go to the cinema with her mum.

Once we'd dropped Rita off we decided to go for an Indian meal. We thought we'd try The Jewel In The Crown since it had been voted best restaurant in Aberdeen several years in a row and neither of us had ever been there. The Jewel had a private car park for customers, so we headed straight to it in the Fiesta. Naturally, we had popadoms with chutney, Alan's starter was mushroom bhaji, mine vegetable samosa, Alan had a spinach-and-potato curry with rice and nan, I had vegetable korma with rice and chappati. This was washed down with Kingfisher lager. We ate and talked about the places we'd been together: Alan was quite adamant that as long as he and Dudley were doing their double act, then we'd only visit historic monuments K. L. Callan name-checked in *69 Things to Do with a Dead Princess*. I lamented that this necessitated missing a number of very moody sites that were sometimes only a few hundred yards from the places we were visiting. I singled out New Craig, next to the Loanhead of Daviot circle, and the Balblair stone in the wood beside Midmar Kirk, as sites we really must visit after Dudley had been executed as Alan's divine substitute.

By the time the dessert arrived, Alan was talking about *The Rings of Saturn* by W. G. Sebald. My companion considered this to be one of the worst travel books he had ever read. Sebald was a Professor of Modern German

Literature at the University of East Anglia in Norwich. This overpaid hack had taken the train from his academic base in Norfolk to the Suffolk border and then written an account of his travels south along the coast. Among other things, Sebald claimed to have difficulty imagining that tourists and business travellers would choose to visit Lowestoft. As Alan observed, it was through this type of half-baked rhetorical trick that the voyeuristic professor attempted to place himself outside the social system that his snobbish comments demonstrated he would never escape by dint of his own efforts.

Alan castigated Sebald for telling the reader very little about Suffolk, and what he did have to say never rising above the level of clichés and inanities. Having stopped at the village of Middleton to visit his friend 'the writer' Michael Hamburger, Sebald not only considered it worth recounting that in the kitchen there were piles of Jiffy bags awaiting re-use, he even provided a photograph of them. Alan was scathing about this example of 'anecdotal information' from Sebald's book, observing that one would imagine most writers are sent a good number of books – some for review, others as tokens of friendship, and yet more that may have been purchased by post for the purposes of research – and that many an author would save the Jiffy bags these books arrived in for re-use when they were mailing their own works to worthy and not-so-worthy recipients. After all, it was well known that most writers subsist on low incomes and that padded envelopes are expensive.

Over coffee the conversation moved on to Napoleon's *How to Make War*. Having talked about Suffolk, which was heavily fortified with Martello towers at a time when the British Government feared that Bonaparte would attempt to invade their dominion, Alan's thoughts had turned naturally enough to the little corporal who'd transformed himself into

a dictator. My companion possessed a recent English translation of Napoleon's military maxims and he considered it
to be the greatest manual on the art of seduction never
written. Later when I skimmed the book I quickly saw
how Alan had applied its lessons not only to the earthy
relationship he enjoyed with me, but also in his dealings
with other women. What Alan had discovered – or to
put it more accurately, rediscovered – was that theory
was not the practice of seduction. Indeed, those whose
experience in the art of seduction was limited to the realm
of theory did not even make good theoreticians. It is not
enough to theorise the art of seduction, this art must be
practised. However, for the practice to be effective it must
be historically informed. To reduce Alan's rich insights to
a few words, the rake must constantly reforge the passage
between the theory and practice of seduction. Ultimately,
the seducer must be seduced by their art, so that the senses
may become theoreticians. Strangely enough, Alan always
insisted that it was the smells he gave off before bathing
that proved he was not only a master strategist but also a
cunning tactician.

Between leaving the Jewel In The Crown and arriving at
Union Grove, I asked Alan what he'd read about Grampian
stone circles apart from *69 Things to Do with a Dead
Princess* and *The Stone Circle: Gordon's Early History*.
Once we'd carted Dudley up to his flat, Alan showed me
A Guide to the Stone Circles of Britain, Ireland and Brittany
by Aubrey Burl and *The Modern Antiquarian* by Julian
Cope. Alan said he was working on a bibliography of books
about stone circles in north-east Scotland and would provide
me with a copy once he'd made a few additions.[9] That night
he restricted himself to being scathing about Julian Cope's
contribution to deforestation. It wasn't difficult to see why
Alan disliked the faded pop singer's hippie mysticism and

obsession with the Mother Goddess. The book was filled with snapshots of Cope and his family standing by stones in leopardskin dresses and other inappropriate gear, the pages were luridly coloured and the author's drug-addled brain appeared incapable of producing coherent thought. Worst of all, Cope included a chapter entitled 'Fifty-Nine Stone Circles in Aberdeenshire' and not only were several of the sites he mentioned actually located in Banffshire, he rated Dunnideer above Bennachie simply because this poxy hill reminded him of Glastonbury Tor! All things considered, *The Modern Antiquarian* was a dog's dinner of a book.

Alan read me numerous examples of Cope's inept prose, chuckling along as he did so. Growing bored, I exposed and then fingered my cunt. Eventually Alan pushed his prick into my dripping wet hole. He evidently had great experience in fucking. I never knew anyone to fuck with such scientific deliberation. He made every stroke tell to the uttermost. He would slowly draw out his prick until the tip of the glans only rested between the lips, and then with equal deliberation drive it slowly back, making its ridge press firmly against the upper creases of my vagina as it passed into my cunt. Then when the whole length was enclosed, and my belly seemed full of it, he would gently work it about from side to side causing the big round head to rub deliciously on the sensitive mouth of my womb.

On reaching orgasm, we both groaned with excess of pleasure and my cunt tingled round his palpitating tool as the life flood darted from the opposite sources of delight in reciprocating streams of unctuous spunk. Alan lay back to recover his breath and rest himself after his exertion, but when he saw me wiping my wet receiver with my handkerchief, he asked me to perform the same kind office for him. I willingly complied, and kneeling at his side, took his soft and moistened prick into my hands and tenderly wiped it all round, then stooping forward, I pressed my lips on its flowing tip. This position elevated my anus, and Alan proceeded at once to avail himself of it. Throwing my dress over my back, he moved me towards him until my naked bum was almost opposite his face, then spreading my thighs, he opened the lips of my quim with his fingers, played about the clitoris, and having moistened his finger in my cunt, pushed it into my arsehole. I rather enjoyed this display of my anal charms. So while I fondled Alan's prick and moulded his balls, he played with the crannies and fissures of my backside.

Then getting me to straddle directly over him, Alan made me stoop until my cunt rested on his mouth. All the lustful feelings of my nature became excited as I felt his warm breath blowing aside the hairs of my sex, and his pliant tongue winding around my clitoris, playing between my nymphae and exploring the secret passage inside. But when he went on to the nether entrance, and I felt the titillation of his tongue amid its sensitive creases, the sluices of pleasure burst open and I became conscious of that melting sensation that told me I had come once again.

Soon after my second orgasm I fell asleep on the sofa. At some point Alan led me semi-conscious through to the bedroom where I was undressed and ushered beneath the sheets. That night I dreamt that I was back in Budapest. Dudley took me to a gypsy bar called The Blue Elephant. Inside the air was thick with smoke. There were guys sitting around broken tables on broken chairs. Some of them were singing, others were playing chess. The place wasn't crowded. There weren't many women although the two bar staff were female. Dudley ordered Cselenye. Cherry brandy. His Hungarian accent was very good. I stared vacantly at some stained wall tiling and a huge poster of a holiday resort I couldn't identify. I didn't particularly care for Cselenye but I guess the regulars did since it was a staple of the sparsely stocked bar. Alan was standing outside on the street. When we left the bar he assaulted his dummy, overcame all resistance and left Dudley lying in a pool of vomit.

Alan took me to the airport and we caught a plane to London. We weaved through passport control without a hitch but got held up by Dudley as we went through customs. The dummy had assumed a military bearing and took great exception to the books stuffed into Alan's suitcase. A copy of Compton MacKenzie's *Whisky Galore* was held aloft and loud demands were made as to why it had not been declared. Alan explained that he'd only used the book as a counterweight to his interests in the east, that MacKenzie was a beacon from the past whose Highland and Island romps provided a perfect counterpoint to contemporary East-Coast writers like Duncan McLean. Of course, MacKenzie's narratives were sentimental and rambling but they had a certain chutzpah. Alan said he'd long puzzled over why the Western Isles had remained bastions of Bible-bashing fundamentalism while in Orkney and Shetland people had become more easy-going about religious observance. MacKenzie had given Alan the key to this enigma. The rivalry between Catholic and Protestant islands fuelled the religious impulse in the west.

As Alan stood and argued with the dummy over the rights and wrongs of failing to declare *Whisky Galore*, visions were flashing through my mind. It was not so much I as Alan who was back in Budapest. He was wandering through Gozsdu udvar, a series of linked courtyards running between Dob utca and Király utca. The architecture was decaying but these courtyards gave an authentic taste of the old Jewish quarter. At ground level the buildings were still in use as shops and workshops but the apartments above were deserted, their windows smashed. The occupied premises were shuttered against the twilight and rain was falling. Alan was walking in slow motion through the smell of decaying plaster. He was examining old bricks, peering through barred windows. The dummy emerged dressed in a black flight jacket from the night watchman's office, a guard dog straining on the lead he held in his plastic hand. Alan unbuttoned the fly of his black Levi's and pissed on the hound's snout. When the urine hit the dog it dissolved. I was back at customs and Alan countered the dummy's claim that MacKenzie was an anti-modernist by pointing out that the author had been an early enthusiast of the gramophone. Dudley confiscated Alan's books but let us go.

The dream ended with images of Dudley's body bobbing about lifelessly in the Danube. Alan was lurking in the shadows and when I tried to escape from him the streets transformed themselves into a stone labyrinth. Alan chased me through winding alleyways and whenever I succeeded in running far ahead, I'd be confronted by the water with Dudley bobbing in the churning foam.

EIGHT

I DON'T remember when I woke up, how many cups of coffee I drank at breakfast or whether Alan and I made love before we rose. However, I do know that Alan drove me out to the university and waited for me in the canteen while I had a tutorial. At first my professor was angry with me for skipping classes but through an astute use of the conversations I'd had with Alan about literature, I managed to convince him that I hadn't been wasting my time. I imagined the professor laying a hand on my leg and running it up under my skirt. Daydreams of this type helped pass the time, although my tutor was actually far too staid to even consider being unfaithful to his wife. Eventually I escaped from my professor's office and Alan drove me to the Donside Tesco superstore. With Dudley seated mutely between us, we had a fry-up in the café. We trailed around the store and Alan grabbed a bag of donuts.

Having disposed of my tutorial as a topic of conversation in the car, our verbal exchanges in Tesco were devoted to other subjects. I suggested that we should visit all the supermarkets in Aberdeen and treat these excursions in much the same way as our trips to stone circles. Alan insisted that it would be difficult to have sex in those stores that lacked customer toilets. I told him that he was missing my point, which was poetic, he had to imagine himself living 3000 years from now and pretend he was visiting ruins. My companion complained this was an impossibility since the logistics of supermarket construction meant the buildings would not survive for this length of time. Such an over-literal response was uncalled for and I eventually persuaded Alan that after leaving Tesco we should travel on to Norco in Kittybrewster. In the meantime, as we queued to pay for the donuts, we talked of books.

Alan insisted that if I was to continue reading the contemporary literature he was rapidly discarding, I should give *The Biography of Thomas Lang: A Novel* by Jonathan Buckley some serious consideration. This text, Alan added slyly, cried out to be described as a work of literature. Taking the form of a series of letters, the novel demonstrated – in a manner not entirely dissimilar to some of the essays in Derrida's *Writing and Difference* or certain works by Wyndham Lewis such as *Enemy of the Stars* – that in order to approach truth, one must simultaneously appear to veer away from it. It should go without saying that language is a tricky thing and that honesty has always hidden itself in lies. Alan praised Buckley for abandoning 19th-century notions of literary depth and said that like many famous modernists and post-modernists, this author's prose was the return at a higher level of pre-modern forms.

Buckley's book is only a novel if one accepts the contradiction of giving this title to a prose work whose central subject eludes it, and not only because the Thomas Lang of the title is dead. As I have already said, the book takes the form of a series of letters, the majority of them being between Michael Dessauer and Christopher Lang. The former is the would-be biographer of a concert pianist called Thomas Lang, the latter the dead man's brother. From the start the book is dialectical in structure, but this is a dialectic of lack. Michael Dessauer is quite unable to make a harmonious whole out of the contradictory testimony he gathers about his subject. Indeed, even the reliability of this material is brought into question since at one point Christopher Lang admits to pranking his correspondent by fabricating letters in his brother's hand.

At times Buckley's game of hide and seek with the reader becomes tiresome and Alan insisted the novelist clearly intended to exhaust his audience. Viz expedients such as providing descriptions of a series of banal photographs allegedly taken by Thomas Lang. These prosaic transcriptions so self-consciously recalled techniques deployed in the French *nouveau roman* that Alan didn't hesitate to cite them as absolutely his favourite sequence in the book. Alan was predisposed to seek out the unoriginal in any work and I strongly suspected it was the fact that he could compare various literary biographies unfavourably with Buckley's novel that led him to praise *Thomas Lang* as a book. Alan's most immediate targets in regard to this were *The Quest for Corvo: An Experiment in Biography* by A. J. A. Symons and *Frank Harris* by Hugh Kingsmill.

Baron Corvo, aka Frederick Rolfe, was a Grub Street hack and shameless paedophile. Although Rolfe received praise from the likes of D. H. Lawrence, book sales long eluded him. Alan liked the first seven chapters of Symons' biography of Corvo, which provided a series of contradictory portraits from different pens. Corvo the brilliant but unrecognised novelist, Rolfe the impostor and con man who'd falsely assumed an aristocratic title, Corvo the dissolute pederast and pander, Rolfe the high-minded inventor and convert to the Catholic faith. After a brilliant opening section Symons attempted to resolve the contradictions he'd so breathlessly delineated. To Alan this was worse than simply tedious, it was a capitulation to the bourgeois notion of a centred subject. His problems with Hugh Kingsmill's *Frank Harris* were of the same order.

Alan loved the early parts of the book where Kingsmill relied on Harris' unreliable and often quite contradictory accounts of his life. He particularly relished the account of Harris travelling home to Europe from America, both westwards across the Pacific and eastwards over the Atlantic, so that he might meet himself in Paris. But once Harris had achieved fame and there were reliable sources for the life of this liar, braggart, charlatan and *bon viveur*, Alan found the sense of certainty that crept into Kingsmill's account mind-numbingly boring.

Nevertheless, Alan considered comparisons of the careers of Frank Harris and Baron Corvo instructive. Harris, Alan was convinced, proved that those afflicted with a bourgeois mentality read books on the basis of who the author was rather than what they wrote. Following Hegel, this was a vice that my companion viewed as more common among critics than the general public. Both men saw the latter as being more generous in their outlook and attitudes. Harris was a literary success as long as he was able to make a go of his society marriage, an alliance to which he'd also hitched his ambition to become the English Bismarck. Inevitably, Harris attached himself to the wrong members of the Conservative Party. Kingsmill correctly characterises his subject's views as those of a Tory anarchist and Harris got no further in politics than various other reactionary scribblers who posed as men of action. Although a sad skunk like Ernst Jünger was both younger than Harris and to the right of him politically, it is not simply coincidence that the 'intellectual' Führer of national bolshevism has been insightfully described as a Prussian anarchist.

By the time Alan got around to discussing this with me, we were buying a pint of milk in the Co-op Superstore in Kittybrewster. As we rolled through the check-out the conversation moved on to the fifth volume of *My Life and*

Loves by Frank Harris. Maurice Girodias of the Olympia Press in Paris had acquired the rights to this book from the author's widow for a considerable sum. Alexander Trocchi was employed to rewrite what there was and construct the rest of the book. Sixty-five per cent of the final text was original prose by Trocchi and the rest notes by Harris worked up into a publishable form. Trocchi completed the book in ten days and since he considered Harris bombastic, used it as an opportunity to lampoon and parody the Tory anarchist. The result was good enough to fool all the literary experts who'd gone over the book in the five years before the hoax was revealed. Alan considered this faked autobiography to be the best of Trocchi's porn novels and the only work 'by' Harris that he would even consider recommending to a friend. It certainly bettered Kingsmill's biography in giving a truly fictional portrait of the man.

However, Alan did not consider *My Life and Loves: Fifth Volume* to be Trocchi's best literary hoax, despite greatly appreciating the fact that this activist hipster had notched up seven porn books against only two 'serious' novels. Trocchi created his best fakes in the 60s, when he turned to book dealing as a means of supporting his smack habit. Since by this time there was a demand for his 'original' manuscripts, Trocchi met it by copying out his already published books in longhand. Alan thought this was an excellent jape and it helped him forgive if not entirely overlook the lapses into conventional literary tropes in Trocchi's porn books. According to Alan, Trocchi was at his best in *Cain's Book* and the faked final volume of *My Life and Loves*. In *Cain's Book* Trocchi had expended a great deal of effort and created a genuinely experimental work of literature, whereas the Frank Harris hoax rocked because it was as badly written and sloppy as the gibberings of any other hack pornographer. Working for money, Trocchi had achieved the genuine pulp writer's trance, something infinitely superior to the automatic writing of the surrealists.

As he drove me to the Safeway on King Street, Alan was ranting about *Thongs*, another of Trocchi's dirty books. *Thongs* was set in Glasgow and at its worst came across as the last gasp of the proletarian novel. Trocchi's depictions of razor kings and Gorbals slums substituted the rhetoric of realism for the strange alchemy of the word and in this fashion patronised the working class. As the story progressed, it degenerated into a litany featuring all the usual claptrap about secret societies dedicated to dominance and submission. Alan insisted that if one really had to read this type of crap it was much better to stick to *The Story of O*. *Thongs* reveals Trocchi himself as a masochist, not because of his loving descriptions of cunnilingus or the fact that his narrator ultimately submits quite willingly to being crucified, but because enough craft has gone into the prose to exorcise the repetitious frenzy so beloved by sadists. Masochists of Trocchi's type are drawn towards art with its frozen tableaux, the sadist prefers the banality of the truly pornographic.

Alan bought some chocolate biscuits in Safeway and got very angry when I said we couldn't go across the street to my bedsit for refreshments. I was embarrassed, my pad was overflowing with the books Alan had been off-loading. At the time of the incidents I am relating I didn't have Alan's old Trocchi books but they are before me now and as literary remains they really are very instructive.

Although Alan didn't like to admit it, he'd spent the late 70s reading through much of the John Calder backlist. This had led him from Samuel Beckett, William Burroughs and Alexander Trocchi on to French writers such as Alain Robbe-Grillet, Marguerite Duras, Claude Simon and Nathalie Sarraute. It therefore isn't surprising that his copy of *Cain's Book* was a British first edition hardback published by John Calder in 1963 and purchased by Alan 15 years later when he was still that mythical beast, 'a teenager'. Alan's copy of *Young Adam*, also purchased secondhand in the late 70s was a Pan paperback with a classic 60s cover. His copies of Trocchi's porn books demonstrated that his interest in this writer was perhaps more tenacious than he cared to admit. There were Olympia Press editions of *My Life and Loves: Fifth Volume* and *Helen and Desire*, that had been acquired secondhand in the early 80s. Alan had purchased a paperback copy of *Sappho of Lesbos* when it was reissued by Star in 1986. The copies of *The Carnal Days of Helen Seferis*, *School For Sin* and *White Thighs* were paperback reissues put out by the American porn publisher Masquerade Books in the early 1990s. *Thongs* had proved even more elusive, Alan had to wait until Blast Books reissued it in 1994 to obtain his own copy, although he'd read it in the British Library some time in the 1980s. Alan also brandished a copy of *Invisible Insurrection of a Million Minds: A Trocchi Reader*, edited by Andrew Murray Scott and put out by Polygon Books in 1991. Although he possessed a number of the books Trocchi had translated, Alan didn't own a copy of the poetry collection *Man At Leisure* and professed himself uninterested in Trocchi's verse.

After much arguing I got my way and rather than going to my pad for refreshments, Alan drove to Asda at the Bridge o' Dee where we made good use of the customer café. By this time Alan was back onto the subject of *Thongs*. He insisted the description it contained of Glasgow as Scotland's grey city was utterly misguided. Anyone who knew the whole of Scotland – and here it's important to remember that Trocchi spent very little of his adult life in Scotland – realised that Aberdeen was the country's grey city since it was built of grey granite. The materials used to build Glasgow were more varied than those on which Aberdeen had been founded. Given that Aberdeen is on the East Coast, Trocchi's claim that Scotland's West-Coast towns are grey and Glasgow the greyest of the lot becomes even more ridiculous. On the evidence of *Thongs* alone, Trocchi's knowledge of Scotland was no more convincing than his sentimental picture of the Gorbals. Alan therefore considered it bizarre that Trocchi's London publisher John Calder singled out this section of *Thongs* as exhibiting literary merit in an essay he contributed to a special number of the *Edinburgh Review* dedicated to the writer.

After downing a cuppa we whizzed around Asda and Alan picked up a couple of ready meals before we hotfooted it to the Bridge o' Dee Sainsbury's. It was at this point that Alan linked his discussion of Trocchi back to *The Biography of Thomas Lang* by mentioning that Trocchi's father had been a concert pianist. It is alleged that Trocchi had relatives who were high up in the Vatican and regardless of whether this is true, the influence of this institution was on open display in *Thongs*. The secret society described in the book with its Holy Pain Father, Pain Cardinals, Grand Painmasters and beneath them ordinary Painmasters and Painmistresses, is clearly modelled on the Catholic Church. Alan thought that by inverting the religious superstitions of his family, Trocchi ended up reproducing the very thing he wished to destroy. The exercise was every bit as futile and reactionary as the so-called Black Masses of Satanists. Indeed, the Vatican was more likely to be damaged by over-fervent converts than Trocchi. In relation to this, Alan specifically mentioned the distasteful sexualised descriptions of a five-year-old prince in Frederick Rolfe's pathetic fantasy *Hadrian the Seventh*.

Returning to the main thrust of his argument, Alan

broached the nature of the relationship between *Thongs* and *Young Adam*. Both books featured characters rejoicing in the surname Gault. In *Thongs* the razor king John Gault is known as the werewolf of the Gorbals. In *Young Adam*, Leslie Gault, an older male character is impotent and the surname is mentioned only once in the entire narrative. For all its faults, Alan insisted that *Thongs* was of some interest when read alongside Trocchi's two literary books. There was even a curious almost stream-of-consciousness passage in the novel when the female narrator is raped and imprisoned in a brothel. Because *Thongs* is a very uneven and unsatisfactory work, it is a useful tool for anyone wanting to unpack Trocchi's artfully crafted depiction of proletarian Glasgow in *Young Adam*.

While purchasing sour-cream Pringles in Sainsbury's, Alan insisted that since Trocchi was for a time a member of the Situationist International, it made perfect sense to read his work dialectically, *Thongs* rubbing up against and ultimately sabotaging *Young Adam* and even *Cain's Book*. Trocchi, like many other members of the SI, appeared to come from the upper echelons of the bourgeoisie. Alan insisted that the fact that Guy Debord and Alex Trocchi were rebelling against their privileged backgrounds in no way negated the fruits of that revolt and it was thus more than simply unfortunate that many of those in the media appeared unable to distinguish the Situationist International's Hegelian Marxism from mere anarchism. While Trocchi was not as rigorous as Debord in elaborating his theoretical positions, those who had not encountered left-communism in all its originality nor understood the nature of its break with the Third International would never grasp the political background to Trocchi's work, nor the ways in which he was driven to continually reforge the passage between theory and practice.

Alan off-loaded his collection of political books and journals several years before I met him and when he moved on to topics of this type I often found it difficult to follow him. Jacques Camatte was one of the pivotal theorists in this area as far as Alan was concerned, and while I have managed to obtain a number of works by this writer in translation much of the material can only be read in either French or Italian. I have never succeeded in following the lines of argument that caused Camatte to turn from Bordiga's brand of super-Leninism to a position where capital was viewed as having escaped human control and thus dominated a universal human class.[10] Since I am not really qualified to summarise the words that poured from Alan's mouth as he drove from the Bridge o' Dee to Bennachie, I shall omit any further description of them. However, it occurs to me that there is one other thing I need to record about Alan's commentary on Trocchi. He considered it hilarious that in *My Life and Loves: Fifth Volume* there was a dig at Marx for having identified the proletarians rather than the bohemians as those who would enjoy true freedom.

Once we reached Bennachie, Alan announced that it was the most famous and popular mountain in north-east Scotland. He explained that this fact was easily accounted for. The graceful outline of the mountain; its standing comparatively alone, and being thus discernible and prominent from all points; the magnificent views to be obtained from its summits; and the easiness of access, all contributed to render Bennachie familiarly known even to those who are not given to mountain climbing. Situated in the Garioch, between the Don and the Gadie, its principal tops, from east to west are Mither Tap 1698 feet, Craig Shannoch 1600 feet, Oxen Craig 1733 feet, Watch Craig 1619 feet, Hermit Seat 1564 feet and Black Hill 1412 feet.

Since it rose 1000 feet above the surrounding countryside,

Bennachie was visible from many of the sites I'd visited with Alan. It stood, black and brooding, dominating the landscape. Mither Tap, the second highest peak was actually the most prominent since the land fell away more sharply there than at Oxen Craig, which rose above it. While Alan can quite fairly be characterised as an ardent admirer of *69 Things to Do with a Dead Princess*, he considered the text deficient in that the only Bennachie peak visited was Mither Tap, and that by the sheerest route. We had decided to take a day off from testing the veracity of Callan's work and so Dudley was left behind in the car while we explored the full extent of the mountain. Our first ascent was of Mither Tap since this is the most popular and most frequently visited of the peaks and the one we already knew. The distance between Mither Tap and Oxen Craig was about a mile and a quarter. At Oxen Craig the view was most extensive and although the day was not perfectly clear, we easily made out many distant mountain peaks. Lochnagar, Ben Avon, Beinn a' Bhuird and Ben Rhinnes were all lightly covered in snow, while Mount Keen, Morven, Clochnaben, Mount Battock, Hill of Fare, Back of the Gabrach, Tap o' Noth and many lesser hills were seen in the nearer distance. There was a brief shower once we reached Oxen Craig but it soon cleared.

Below Garbit Tap, midway between the tops we visited, but a little to the south, there is an old disused quarry and adjoining it a ruined smiddy. For a number of years in the 19th century this was the abode of William Jamieson, a character known locally as the Heddie Craw o' Bennachie. Jamieson was a social outcast and he acted the bogie man to all the children round about so well that for a time his celebrity spread outside the immediate area. We made our descent to Beeches Well and then skirted around the base of the mountain and back to the car. After our hill-walking we were hungry so we charged back to Aberdeen on the

A96. Once the car was parked outside Alan's flat on Union
Grove we walked the short distance to Pappagallos on
Holborn Street. There's nothing like a light but perfectly
prepared Italian meal for igniting the fires of passion and
over coffee we agreed to repair to Union Grove for a
horny-arsed fuck.

Alan's flat was much sparser than the first time I'd visited
it. There were no longer any books in the bedroom. Indeed
all the furniture had been removed and the clothes he still
possessed were heaped up in a corner. There was no longer
a bed, just a mattress on the floor with a rough blanket
thrown over it. Alan went through to the kitchen to fetch
some whisky and some time later returned with a bottle. The
Laphroaig was placed on the floor and my love descended
upon me like shadows at dusk enveloping a pretty country
hamlet. His roseate limbs seemed floating in celestial light.
I stretched up my arms and told my love how delightful
it was to be with him now. I felt his dear hands groping
between the lips of my palpitating sex. I opened my thighs
and heaved my bottom as I murmured that Alan should feel
up my cunt, how hot it was in its longing for his prick. His
fingers tickled me nicely but it was his cock I wanted, his
cock encased to its very root in my maidenhood.

Alan turned me over and lay upon my back. He slipped a
blindfold over my eyes and then drew back so that he might
drain his dram. He moved forward and poured my dram
down my throat. I could no longer see Alan but I could
feel him, his arm around me and his warm body pressing
me deliciously. He put his prick in my hand. It was large
and stiff. Letting the head pass through my fingers, I drew
back the soft covering skin. I felt it bound in my hand. I
told Alan to put it inside me as I drew his root towards my
cunt. I told him I was longing for the plunge and that my
cunt was burning with desire. I felt the head rub between

my moist lips. I felt it press on the heated orifice. I heaved up and it slipped in. I let out a little scream of pleasure as it passed up my sex extending each humid fold and sensitive crease of the damp passage. The prick felt larger than usual and I was suffocated with rapture at the way Alan fucked me, since it was rare for him to treat me so roughly.

Alan rammed home his prick with desperate energy and with a low moaning cry shot forth a torrent of boiling spunk. I felt my cunt filled to overflowing. I knew it was bubbling out at the sides. I passed my hand over Alan. He had grown larger and heavier since we'd last fucked. His skin was less soft than I remembered. Then Alan, or at least at that point I still believed the man to be Alan, stood up. He moved away and then it was Alan who placed his arms around me. I found out later why Alan had taken so long to get our whiskies. He'd fetched the big brute of a student from downstairs. The student had hidden outside the bedroom until Alan had me blindfolded, then he slipped in and took my love's place. Realising more or less what must have happened, I felt even hornier than usual when Alan shoved his root up my buttered bun. I screamed at Alan not to beat about the bush, he was to fuck me hard. Alan obeyed my instructions and minutes later we'd both come, my insides flooded with spunk once again. Alan got up and poured our guest a dram, I fell back against a pillow and moments later I was asleep.

That night I dreamt that all about me there were hills which garnished their proud heights with stately trees and beneath a humble valley comforted with a silver river, meadows, emerald with all sorts of eye-pleasing flowers and thickets, which, being lined with most pleasant shade, were witnessed so by the cheerful disposition of many well-tuned birds. Each pasture was stored with sheep feeding in sober security, while pretty lambs with bleating oratory proclaimed the peace and comfort of this arcadia. A shepherd boy was piping as though he would never grow old. A young shepherdess sat knitting and singing, her voice comforting her hands and her hands keeping time with the heavenly music she was spinning. The houses of this valley were scattered about, no two being one by the other, and yet not so far off that distance barred mutual succour. A show, as it were, of accompanied solitude and of civil wildness. The scene picturesque and in marked contrast to the black sublimnity of Bennachie, whose pink granite quickly darkens upon exposure to the elements.

NINE

I AWOKE to find Dudley ravishing me, or rather Alan woke me as he helped his ventriloquist's dummy simulate rape. A large dildo had been screwed into Dudley's groin and Alan was attempting to ram this up my queynt. I screamed, Alan placed a hand over my face. Shortly afterwards I found myself gagged. I struggled but Alan, who was determined Dudley should have his way with me, had tied my limbs to the four corners of the bed. At some point Alan picked up a short riding crop and beat me. After these stimulations, Dudley's extension slipped easily inside me. I don't recall when I'd first confessed to Alan that I had fantasies about being raped by the dummy but he'd listened attentively and the sympathetic way he catered for my sexual needs was very pleasing. After Dudley had exercised his detachable part, Alan brought his moist lips down upon my steaming cunt so that he might worship there. He worked his tongue around my swollen clitoris and thrust two fingers up towards my womb. Eventually he bit the fleshy part he'd so excited with his lingua and an orgasm of immense power and duration shuddered through my heaving bulk.

Alan got on top of me and plunged the chief implement for the propagation of our species into my welcoming vulva. This felt good but what I really wanted was another beating. Alan tore the gag from my mouth and I told him to tan my backside and then fuck me the Greek way. I hadn't even finished uttering this request as Alan began unfastening my bonds. Roughly, very roughly, he rolled me onto my stomach and then began to horsewhip me. Alan, who I momentarily misidentified with Dudley, understood my true nature and my most secret desires far better than I did at that time. Not only did he bring out increasingly deep red blushes as he bruised my buttocks, he worked the crop up and down my legs and back as well. As Alan explained to me later, a single area of flesh that is whipped soon goes numb and the slave being chastised feels little pain. Since I was seeking more than mere humiliation my pleasure was maximised by enlarging the area of my distress. Eventually Alan threw the crop down and mounted my chaffed buttocks. Oh joy to feel him burst through the puny resistance offered by my sphincter muscles and plunge up my backside. My partner had made perhaps ten strokes before the sap rose within him and he fell upon my back, smothering me like a collapsing building.

We dozed before rising. As he made breakfast Alan began talking about *Alexander Trocchi: The Making of the Monster* by Andrew Murray Scott. Alan was indifferent about whether Trocchi was well served by this biography, what interested him as a reader was what he could get from the book. The laughs squeezed from filtering Trocchi through the perspectives of Scottish nationalism were both hollow and purely unintentional on Murray Scott's part. Indeed, Andy Scott had so little understanding of his subject that one doubted he had the intellectual capacity to knowingly lie. Dismissable as he was, Alan continued dismissing Murray Scott as we drove to Ellon. We passed through the town and doubled back on ourselves as we laced the four and a half miles by minor roads to South Ythsie stone circle. Alan parked the car at the top of a lane that led down to the monument. He threw Dudley over his shoulders and we took our bearings from a wooden arrow marked with the words 'stone circle'.

The circle had been 'restored' in 1994 on the initiative of a local heritage project, which meant that at the bottom of the lane there was a notice board with information about the stones. We followed the path around a corner and crossed a field of corn where a sign proclaimed 'Cross here'. There were six stones with a mound of earth heaped up around them. The earth was indicative of the problems of restoration, since it was not clear whether those who erected the stones intended to heap earth around them or if this feature was a later addition. The earth mound had been removed more than 100 years ago and recently restored. The main Aberdeen-to-Fraserburgh road was a couple of fields behind us, so there was no danger of anyone using the 'A' route noticing as Alan wedged Dudley in the cleft of the split south-west stone, then got me to jerk him off into the dummy's face.

Once Alan had zipped up he slung Dudley over his shoulders and we made our way back to the car. We were using back roads since they got us closer to where we were going than the arterial routes radiating out from Aberdeen. Our journey towards the Shethin stone circle was circuitous. As he drove Alan talked about Alexander Trocchi's work with the Olympia Press and John de St Jorre's book *The Good Ship Venus: The Erotic Voyage of the Olympia Press*. Of course, Olympia was not simply a pornographic operation, it also published 'serious' works by the likes of Samuel Beckett and Jean Genet when few other English-language publishers would touch them. Alan said he'd known what to expect from de St Jorre from the kick-off, since in his preface this cretin speaks of banned books being burnt in the same way heretics were burnt by religious tyrants. Alan was always quick to denounce the cruel inhumanity of liberal fuckwits who wantonly blurred the lines between human life and the products of a literary culture that had yet to escape its commodity form.

We parked the car beside some cottages that lined up with Shethin stone circle on Alan's Ordnance Survey map. The land sloped upwards and we couldn't see the stones as we trudged through a field of barley. The circle was ruinous, with stones cleared from the field piled up on top of it. Alan threw Dudley over a stone that was still standing and spanked the dummy before we went back to the car. All the way he complained that he couldn't understand why Shethin had been included in *69 Things to do with a Dead Princess*, since in his opinion it didn't merit a visit. Once we were heading north in the Fiesta Alan returned to the subject of de St Jorre's book which he considered boring. Its half-witted author didn't appreciate quite how central Trocchi's role had been in the Olympia Press and didn't give him sufficient space. Instead, there were four chapters dedicated to the litigation over Olympia's mishandling of the rights to *The Ginger Man*, *Lolita* and *Candy*.

Alan complained bitterly about the chapter de St Jorre dedicated to revealing the 'true' identity of the individual who wrote *The Story Of O*, since although he'd read and enjoyed this work he found it hard to believe anyone very much cared who was responsible for it. Equally ridiculous was de St Jorre's desire to explain the work of William Burroughs as if it was in some way difficult. Another wasted chapter that might have been dedicated to various Olympia Press japes like putting out a sci-fi, porn and politics crossover novel entitled *President Kissinger* and issuing a dirty book called *Sir Cyril Black* with a sadistic central character who was based on the right-wing British MP Sir Cyril Black. Being a bourgeois bore de St Jorre dismissed pranks of this type with a few sentences instead of giving them the space they deserved as characteristic examples of the Grub Street mentality.

Eventually Alan turned up a farm lane and parked the car as close as he could to the Aikey Brae stone circle. There were no signs but a path was laid out for visitors. First we crossed a field, then we made our way through a little wood, the path marked out with a pebble boarder. On the other side of the trees we found the circle. Only four of the upright stones are now standing. Six uprights have been overthrown and lie about in fragments, great and small. The stones are of diorite, gneiss and granite. Gneiss is the rock of the district, granite is found within half a mile, but there is no diorite rock visible in the neighbourhood, though ice-borne blocks may be seen in the fences of nearby fields. On the south side of the circle, lying east and west, is a vast diorite stone, 14 feet and 9 inches in length, five feet and nine inches in height, the same in width and about 20 tons in weight. The upper surface presents a considerable plane, the whole forming a substantial platform on which half a dozen persons may stand with ease. This recumbent is closely flanked by two of the largest of the uprights, the one on the east, still standing, being six feet wide and more than seven feet high, while the one on the west is six feet eight inches wide and nine feet high. The latter is broken down, but its form and dimensions are easily ascertained from its huge fragments. Right and left of those two flanking stones were two others, also of great size, being respectively nine feet and six feet in height.

Since we were well hidden from view, the trees obscuring the nearest sections of road, I began to strip. Alan sat Dudley up on the recumbent and proceeded to give me a slow handclap, every now and then throwing his voice so that it appeared the dummy was telling him to shut up and encouraging me to hurry up and get my kit off. In this fashion Alan argued with Dudley for the best part of 20 minutes. Once I was starkers Alan told me to spread my legs and piss. I did so and when I opened the floodgates, Alan shoved his hands into my fast flowing waters. Once I'd finished Alan inspected the sleeves of his jacket. He was furious when he noticed a few drops of urine. I was ordered to lick them off. Then I was made to stand with my arms spread against the recumbent and take my punishment.

I could feel the blush blooming across my buttocks after the first hot slap, which was quickly followed by a second stinging blow, then a third, fourth and fifth. At this point a couple in their 20s emerged from the trees. Alan told them to strip and I have to admit that I was surprised when they obeyed. Alan ordered me and the girl to rub our pussies together but after no more than a few minutes pulled us apart. I was set up on the recumbent next to Dudley so that the boy could lick me out while his girlfriend gave Alan a blow job. After we'd had our orgasms, Alan took Dudley from the recumbent and got the boy to stretch out on that great flat stone. Then he made the girl lie on top 69-style and watched them bring each other off. After I'd dressed we exchanged phone numbers with this couple so that further fun might be arranged at ancient monuments. The submissives were still frolicking bollock-naked amongst the stones when we left with Dudley sprawled over Alan's back.

Having installed Dudley safely on the back seat of the car, Alan mentioned *Paris Interzone: Richard Wright, Lolita, Boris Vian and others on the Left Bank 1946–1960* by James Campbell as a book that covered some of the same ground as *The Good Ship Venus* but was infinitely preferable. A good range of writers were featured and Trocchi was given his due. Unfortunately, as Alan observed, in Trocchi's case simply running through his relationships with other writers wasn't good enough because at the time he edited *Merlin* he was also a member of a little-known avant-garde group called the Lettrist International. Other members included Michele Bernstein, Guy Debord and Gil. J. Wolman. What Campbell did do adequately was demonstrate just how central Trocchi was to the Olympia Press and enough documents were quoted at sufficient length to make his tendency towards pretension and megalomania patently apparent. According to Alan these were the personality traits that made Trocchi a great writer and it is our loss that in this area he was ultimately eclipsed by his friend Debord.

Alan pulled up on the edge of Loudon Wood and Dudley was once more slung across his shoulders. We strolled down the main path before swinging left and then right. Finally we took another right, pushing our way through thick shrubbery and a moment later found ourselves in a clearing. The stone circle before us was larger than that at Aikey Brae, being about sixty feet in diameter, and while the circle itself was larger, the stones comprising it, judging from those still remaining, were smaller. The recumbent was not so massive as that Aikey Brae but there was a strong similarity in the general outline of the two circles, as well as in their positions. Only two uprights and a flanker were still standing, the one to the west – the largest – being seven feet and two inches above ground. The circle appeared to have consisted of two concentric rings, the inner being about 50 feet in diameter but the whole was in such dilapidated condition that it is not possible to affirm this with certainty. There seemed to have been an attempt to break up some of the stones that had fallen and the ground enclosed by the circle was waterlogged and boggy. Nevertheless, given its setting in a woodland clearing, the monument possessed an eerie dignity.

Alan was all for having more sex but I refused since this would have entailed getting muddy or suffering bruises on the hard surface of the recumbent. Instead we made our way back through the wood with Dudley still slung across Alan's shoulders. We crossed the road our car was parked on, traversed a field and headed up a hill. All the way my companion was complaining that in *69 Things to Do with a Dead Princess* there was a two-hour picnic at the Loudon Wood circle. I pointed out that unlike K. L. Callan we had not enjoyed a clear sky and full moon. Indeed it had clouded over as we made our way to the stanes. Since we were only attempting to test the feasibility of Callan's narrative and in so doing had substituted a dummy weighted with bricks for the corpse of a dead princess, cutting the time we spent at sites was of no consequence. Our goal was only to go over the territory covered in *69 Things to Do with a Dead Princess*. That we were able to do so didn't prove that this picaresque tale was true, merely that there was an outside chance it wasn't false.

Alan was unable to counter the iron logic of my argument, so by the time we reached Auchmachar stone circle, or at least the little that was left of it, he'd quit whingeing. Only two stones remained of what had once been an embanked recumbent circle. Nearby was a ruined Bronze-Age long cairn. These relics were singularly unimpressive so we scampered off the hill towards White Cow Wood. As Alan strode before me with the dummy slung over his shoulder, I could see a perverse logic to tramping around this rich farmland with the corpse of a dead princess. However, given the fences and muddy fields we had to negotiate I was glad that we were merely using a weighted dummy. While Dudley might attract attention, it was quite safe for us to carry out our experiment during the hours of daylight. Had we actually made use of a corpse as K. L. Callan claimed he had done, it would have necessitated copying his modus operandi of visiting these ancient and sacred sites in the dead of night.

We identified Upper Aughnagorth stone circle easily
enough although one of the remaining stones had been
incorporated into a fence and leakage from a water tank
was efficiently bringing about its complete obliteration.
We didn't stop longer than was necessary to take in this
vandalism. Nearby was the White Cow Wood cairn circle.
It is formed of a great number of comparatively small stones,
rising above the ground from one foot to two and a half feet,
and where stones three or four feet in length have been used,
they are laid along their length on the ground, so that in no
case does the height of the encircling stone reach above two
and a half feet. The stones present a clear face on the inside
of the circle but are backed up with earth all round. Thus
the circle is formed practically of a low earthen rampart,
faced on the inside with stones, the tops of the stones rising
sometimes above the rampart, but very often being under
it. A little east of the south, a breach has been made in the
circle, the stones or their fragments being cast outside. The
most remarkable feature of the circle is the tomb or stone
sarcophagus placed a little north of the centre. Its exterior
dimensions are seven feet by five feet and two feet three
inches in height.

We stood admiring the remains of the cairn. All the
smaller stones had been carried away some time in the 19th
century and used in a dike. What remained was spooky,
the wood around us being very thick but inside the circle
the ground was bare and black. Scarcely a vestige of veg-
etation was to be seen among the stones that had proved
too large to cart away for use in the dike, while outside moss, grass and heather grew rank and old, making it appear as if the ring had just been laid bare. My
guess is that it had been recently cleared for archaeological study since there was nothing to suggest we would
find it in this denuded state when we combed through

the relevant passages in *69 Things to Do with a Dead Princess.*

As we were preparing to leave the cairn the rain that had been threatening to come on as we made our way to the wood poured from the sky. We sheltered as best we could among the tress and Alan used this enforced break as an opportunity to talk about H. Montgomery Hyde's *A History of Pornography.* The book would have been perfect background material to Trocchi's work with the Olympia Press had the author resisted plodding through English laws and court cases pertaining to obscenity in such tedious detail. Hyde also made the odd *faux pas* that Alan could not resist denouncing as typically bourgeois. For example, in the second section of his first chapter Hyde suggests only the upper classes were able to read in the 18th century. As Alan pointed out, since the aristocracy and the bourgeoisie were rarely employed in the manufacture of the books they consumed, and since in order to compose type – a skill that formed an integral part of 18th-century book production – one must be able to read, Hyde's statement was patently untrue. Perhaps, Alan allowed generously, this fault arose from Hyde taking the description of printers as the aristocracy of labour too literally. Suffice to say that since Hyde's book was published in the 60s, some space towards the end was devoted to Maurice Girodias and the Olympia Press. Trocchi wasn't mentioned but his novel *White Thighs* was name-checked.

When the rain eased we made our way to the car. Once Dudley had been stashed on the back seat it began to piss down again. The rain drummed out an irregular rhythm that gradually lost its insistence as we drove. The weather had lifted by the time we reached Strichen. We walked along a lane until we came to the ruins of Strichen House. Cutting through a waterlogged field towards the abandoned manor,

I thought of Johnson's sharp dismissal of the stanes we were approaching: 'We dined this day at the house of Mr Frazer of Strichen, who shewed us in his grounds some stones yet standing of a Druidical circle, and what I began to think more worthy of notice, some forest trees of full growth.' Things had changed since that day in August 1773, the circle had been destroyed at least twice only to be re-erected, the final time in the early 1980s after two careful archaeological surveys.

The soil became particularly boggy as we approached the ruined house and we had to edge our way around a large patch of shrubbery, which was the only piece of ground that wasn't completely churned up by the cows that had been driven through the field very recently. As we picked our way I chewed over the few words Boswell devoted to Strichen: 'We set out about nine. Dr Johnson was curious to see one of those structures which northern antiquarians call a Druid's temple. I had a recollection of one at Strichen, which I had seen fifteen years ago; so we went four miles out of our road, after passing Old Deer, and went thither. Mr Frazer, the proprietor, was at home, and shewed it to us. But I had augmented it in my mind; for all that remains is two stones set up on end, with a long one laid upon them, as was usual, and one stone at a little distance from them. That stone was the capital one of the circle which surrounded what now remained. Mr Frazer was very hospitable. There was a fair at Strichen; and he had several of his neighbours from it at dinner.'

Having gone downhill through one field, we next made our way uphill through another, the circle coming into view as we did so. The stones were protected from grazing cattle by a wire fence. Both Alan and I found the stanes disappointing, although it's difficult to say exactly why. Standing as they did atop a small hill, the setting was less impressive than a good number of the other sites we had visited. Likewise, knowing the history of the circle didn't help. I appreciated the trouble different people had gone to in re-erecting the stones at various times, but knowing the frequency and extent of their disturbance robbed the romantic in me of certain sublime excitements I associate with the antique. Perhaps the sheer accessibility of the circle repelled me. It was the only recumbent in the Buchan area listed in all the local tourist guides. Alan sat Dudley down on a rock and suggested we talk of Boswell and Johnson. I replied it might perhaps be amusing to reprint their accounts of the trip to Scotland side by side, scene by scene, so that their two voices might undercut and rub up against each other. Alan bemoaned the conservatism of the book trade and its perference for running Boswell and Johnson's accounts of their tour back to back.

Heading for the car we were splashed by the odd heavy raindrop. Seconds after we reached the Fiesta, the heavens opened. Our plan had been to head for the Berrybrae stone circle but, given the weather, we decided to visit Fraserburgh. It seemed likely we'd be better able to stay dry while amusing ourselves in a town. It was still pouring when we parked the car, so we walked straight into a café with windows that advertised cappuccino and espresso. The Gaggia machine was brand-new and after we'd sauntered up to the counter and asked for espressos, the waitress looked a little puzzled before suggesting that what we wanted was a cappuccino without the milk. Alan exploded, screaming that there was no such thing as a cappuccino without the milk. The waitress said in that case she didn't know how to make an espresso. Alan yelled that this style of coffee was advertised in the window and that was what we wanted. Eventually the waitress called someone over and got instructions on what to do with the gleaming Gaggia machine in order to produce espresso. We finally got our strong black coffee in two cappuccino mugs filled to the brim.

Given the quantity of espresso we'd been served, the drinks cost very little. Alan smiled and thanked the waitress politely as she handed him some change. He wasn't going to bother explaining the concept of espresso to a pretty girl from a small Scottish town. Life was too short and besides, the bold lines and noble simplicity of the waitress brought to mind the ox-like prose of Ernest Hemingway. Alan sipped his coffee and our conversation flitted from *A Farewell to Arms* to *A Long Time Burning: A History of Literary Censorship in England* by Donald Thomas. The latter tome covered some of the same ground as Hyde's *A History of Pornography* but extended into the political and religious realms, as well as giving space to the merely obscene. Thomas was aware of the problem of boring readers by spending too much time on legal considerations, although there was still more law than Alan cared for. On the plus side Thomas had managed to dig up a number of amusing anecdotes from the annals of State Trials. Among the best was a passage dealing with an attempt in February 1728 to punish the publisher Edmund Curil for issuing politically sensitive works such as *The Memoirs Of John Ker* (a government spy), as well as dirty books such as *Venus In The Cloister* and *Treatise On The Use Of Flogging*: 'This Edmund Curil stood in the pillory at Charing Cross but was not pelted, or used ill; for being an artful, cunning (though wicked) fellow, he had contrived to have printed papers dispersed all about Charing Cross, telling the people, he stood there for vindicating the memory of Queen Anne: which had such an effect on the mob, that it would have been dangerous even to have spoken against him: and when he was taken down out of the pillory, the mob carried him off, as it were in triumph, to a neighbouring tavern.'

Upon finishing our refreshments, we decided to remain in Fraserburgh until such time as it stopped raining. Having had the foresight to bring an umbrella, we took a walk along the harbour, where we saw the fishing fleet. This was the principal source of the town's wealth. Next we took a wander through a number of shop-lined streets but found little to do. It was easy to understand how Fraserburgh had gained such a reputation for heroin abuse. There was good money to be made on the boats and this was reflected in the high prices of the properties advertised by local estate agents. Men would go out to sea for a few weeks' fishing, then come home and get smacked out of their heads. There was fuck-all else to do. We tried going to the library but the local history section was disorganised and Alan couldn't find what he wanted. The moment it stopped raining, we headed back to the car.

Berrybrae was situated six and a half miles south-east of Fraserburgh and we could see the stone circle from the road. Alan threw Dudley across his back and we climbed over a gate and walked through a field to the recumbent stone circle. The stanes were situated in a clump of trees, fenced off so that the cows that grazed close by wouldn't damage them. The cattle had clocked us and, being bored, wandered over to see what we were doing. It was at this point that I noticed one of the 'cows' snorting and marking the earth with a front hoof. Looking for an udder and seeing instead a huge prick, I realised almost immediately that this beast was a bull. I cried out in fear. Alan told me to shut up and stand still. After about ten minutes the cattle lost interest in us and began to wander off. Leaving the protection of the fenced-off monument, we made our way smartly across the field in the opposite direction to the herd.

Alan chuckled over this incident as he drove me back to Aberdeen. He parked the car outside his flat on Union

Grove and we stumbled up the road to a bistro called
The Rendezvous. That night I dreamt I was lost in a
subterranean maze and that, upon reaching the centre, I
was confronted by a white bull, which gored me to death.
I awoke screaming. Alan took me in his arms and before
long we were making sweet love to each other.

TEN

RISING FROM the dead, I kicked Alan out of bed. He'd slept long enough and we had a full day ahead of us. I was eager to get up the road and insisted that rather than having breakfast at home, it would be quicker to get something on the way. We pushed through the heavy traffic on Union Street and then swung north up King Street. Alan wanted to pick up some books from his flat but I insisted he retrieve them on our way back into town. I was eager to get at least as far as Ellon before we stopped. As I drove I told Alan about a book I'd been reading, *A Long Time Burning: A History of Literary Censorship in England* by Donald Thomas. What had impressed me was a section in which the Gothic novel was described as giving socially acceptable expression to the type of sadism and morbid sexuality found in banned pornographic literature. Of course, as Thomas pointed out, Matthew Lewis in *The Monk* overstepped the mark and only escaped prosecution by producing a bowdlerised version of his macabre classic.

I pulled up outside the Safeway at Ellon and we ventured in, hoping to find a café. Alan was horribly disappointed to discover there wasn't even a customer toilet. We left the car where it was and walked to a greasy spoon for a fry-up. As we ate I reflected on the huge changes Ellon had undergone since Boswell and Johnson's visit on Tuesday 24 August 1773. Boswell: 'We set out about eight in the morning, and breakfasted at Ellon. The landlady said to me, "Is not this the great Doctor that is going about through the country?" – I said, "Yes," – "Ay", (said she,) "we have heard of him, I made an errand into the room on purpose to see him. There's something great in his appearance: it is a pleasure to have such a man in one's house; a man who does so much good. If I had thought of it, I would have shewn him a child of mine, who has had a lump on his throat for some time." – "But, (said I,), he is not a doctor of physic." – "Is he an occultist?" said the landlord – "No, (said I,) he is only a very learned man." – Landlord. "They say he is the greatest man in England, except Lord Mansfield." – Dr Johnson was highly entertained with this, and I do think he was pleased too. He said, "I like the exception: to have called me the greatest man in England, would have been an unmeaning compliment: but the exception marked that the praise was in earnest; and in Scotland, the exception must be Lord Mansfield, or Sir John Pringle."'

Johnson, of course, passes over not only this incident but the entire episode of the breakfast in Ellon saying only that 'the road beyond Aberdeen grew more stony, and continued equally naked of all vegetable decoration. We travelled over a tract of ground near the sea, which, not long ago, suffered a very uncommon and unexpected calamity. The sand of the shore was raised by a tempest in such quantities, and carried to such a distance, that an estate was overwhelmed and lost. Such and so hopeless was the barrenness superinduced, that the owner, when he was required to pay the usual tax, desired rather to resign the ground . . .'

Having run a slice around my plate to mop up the remains of my eggs and beans, I downed the grounds of my coffee and paid the bill. After retrieving my motor from the Safeway car park I cut through the back roads. First we travelled along the B9005 and soon after crossing the Elvie

Burn detoured north to the Candle Stane. We found the standing stone easily enough since it was visible from the road as we trundled along. I parked the car and we paced uphill. The stone was positioned just below the summit of a gentle slope and Bennachie was displayed to magnificent effect in the background. The Candle Stane was massive, no wonder it had never been cleared from the field. While there were no cattle grazing when we visited, I imagined cows rubbing themselves contentedly against this gigantic rock.

I told Alan to drop his pants. Needless to say he had an erection by the time his trousers were around his ankles. I bent my body and took Alan's cock in my mouth. After I'd given his fat, juicy prick a bit of a suck, I leant back against the Candle Stane and twirled my partner around. Once my breasts were pressed against Alan's back my hand snaked around his waist and began to finger his balls. Sunlight glinted against glass and I saw a girl in her late teens standing behind the upper window of a house close to where I'd parked my car. With one hand she pressed a pair of binoculars against her eyes, the flies of her jeans were undone and her other hand was in her panties. I put my hand around Alan's cock and jerked slowly, steadily increasing my tempo. The girl kept time with me, her rhythm changing with mine. My hand was a blur of motion by the time Alan came, the girl collapsed backwards at the same moment, evidently in the throes of orgasm. Alan took five to catch his breath and adjust his clothing. When we got to the car there was a note under one of the wipers. On it was written the name Janet, a telephone number and a message asking us to give advance notice next time we were visiting the Candle Stane.

As we threaded our way back to Ellon, I grew tired of Alan complaining he was missing Dudley and told him to shut up. As far as I was concerned, if my friend wanted a three-way fuck fest, then he should do it with real live pervs. I found his attachment to the ventriloquist's dummy peculiar, to say the least. I also made it clear that I was sick to death of hearing about *69 Things to Do with a Dead Princess*. The book wasn't even coherent. I'd counted the number of sites the author claimed to have visited with the royal corpse and had come up with the figure of 169. Alan defended his favourite work of faction by claiming the title must have been a typo, insisting a one had been lost by the typesetter and that the author obviously intended to call it *169 Things to Do with a Dead Princess*.

When we reached Ellon I pulled up in the Safeway car park and we made our way to a café for coffee. Our cappuccinos were a tad weak. Until the 60s Ellon was just a wee village but with the oil boom it had swelled into a town that was quite literally awash with money. I decided to make things up with Alan after our argument in the car, so I told him that once we got home I was going to call up one of my college friends and make him take his pants down in front of her before ordering him to lick the girl out. This not only got Alan excited, the idea appealed to a woman who overheard our conversation. Her husband was away working on a rig, so we headed back to her place and I watched as Alan shagged the middle-aged wanton.

Alan always enjoyed sex with bored housewives but once we were heading north he began bickering about *69 Things to Do with a Dead Princess*. To cut a long story short, by the time we got to Cruden Bay I'd made it clear that while I was more than happy to visit stone circles, there was no way I'd trot around all the Grampian distilleries and castles allegedly visited by the dead princess. The whole thing was really quite disgusting, since once the corpse was badly decomposed K. L. Callan described decapitating it and ripping out the heart before placing this organ in the royal mouth. These body parts were wrapped in plastic and placed in a rucksack to expedite travel on the castle and malt-whisky trails. Although dismemberment made the incidents described in parts two and three of *69 Things to Do with a Dead Princess* physically possible, the narrative still strained credulity. During the course of this argument we'd got out of the car and ascended the grassy knoll on the north side of Cruden Bay. Reaching the top, we could see Slains Castle half a mile away.

It had been our intention to walk to Slains Castle but there was a rumble of thunder and it began to piss down. The castle had been built at the end of the 16th century and was given a Gothic make-over in the 19th. Brooding blackly above the sea, Slains Castle is said to have provided Bram Stoker with the inspiration to write Dracula. It is perhaps better to pass over what Boswell wrote about the castle since his strength as a writer lay in describing people and social situations, while the sublime was most definitely one of his weak spots. Johnson's comments were brief and lucid. 'We came in the afternoon to Slanes Castle, built upon the margin of the sea, so that the walls of one of the towers seem only a continuation of a perpendicular rock, the foot of which is beaten by the waves. To walk round the house seemed impracticable. From the windows the eye wanders over the sea that separates Scotland from Norway, and when the winds beat them with violence they must enjoy all the terrific grandeur of the tempestuous ocean. I would not for my amusement wish for a storm; but as storms, whether wished or not, will sometimes happen, I may say, without violation of humanity, that I should willingly look out upon them from Slanes Castle.'

We made our way back to the car and, thoroughly soaked, drove to a geological feature known as the Bullers Of Buchan. It is a rock perpendicularly tabulated, united on one side with a high shore, and on the other rising steep to a great height, above the main sea. The top is open, from which may be seen a dark gulf of water which flows into the cavity, through a breach made in the lower part of the enclosing rock. It has the appearance of a vast well bordered with a wall. The edge of the Buller is not wide, and to those that walk around appears very narrow. He that ventures to look downwards sees that if his foot should slip, he must fall from his dreadful elevation upon stones on one side, or into the water on the other. We, however, went round, and were glad when the circuit was completed, for although the rain had eased off, it was a slippery walk.

On going down to the sea, we saw some boats and rowers, and resolved to explore the Buller at the bottom. We entered the arch that the water had made and found ourselves in a place, which, though we could not think ourselves in danger, we could scarcely survey without some recoil of the mind. The basin in which we floated was nearly circular, perhaps 30 yards in diameter. We were enclosed by a natural wall, rising steep on every side, to a height which produced the idea of insurmountable confinement. The interception of all lateral light caused a dismal gloom. Round us was a perpendicular rock, above us the distant sky, and below an unknown profundity of water. If I had any malice against a walking spirit, instead of laying him in the Red Sea, I would condemn him to reside in the Bullers of Buchan.

But terror without danger is only one of the sports of fancy, a voluntary agitation of the mind that is permitted no longer than it pleases. We were soon at leisure to examine the place with minute inspection, and found many cavities which, as the watermen told us, went backwards to a depth which they had never explored. Their extent we had not time to try; for the rain came on hard again and once we'd been let ashore we made our way back to the car.

Upon reaching Peterhead, we immediately sought a café in which to dry out. I asked for two double espressos in a single cup. At first this was refused, the waitress saying she'd never heard of such a thing. Since I persisted in my request it was eventually agreed that I could have my coffee served whatever way I wanted, but that it was on my own head if I fell ill. The waitress and several of her customers stared at me as I slurped the beverage, so I decided to give them something to really talk about. In a loud clear voice I told Alan of a visit I'd once made to Turku Cathedral in Finland. The tombs in several chapels contained the mortal remains of those who'd fought on behalf of Sweden as it oppressed its little neighbour. Several of these imperial mercenaries were Scottish soldiers of fortune or their descendants as was obvious from names such as Cockburn and Wedderburn.

The monument to General Cockburn in Turku Cathedral is particularly striking, the thistle being conspicuous in the carved design. Through all the early history of the Swedish occupation of Finland the deeds of Scots are woven. Families descended from those wandering, warring Scots now form a large part of the Swedish-speaking aristocracy that for long centuries oppressed the Finns and among them one will come across such names as Ramsay, Fraser, Douglas, Montgomery and Hamilton. My little speech did not go down well and I was asked to leave the café, which I did without settling the bill. The rain was easing up and on the way to the car Alan attempted to discuss a biographical work entitled *Antonin Artaud: Blows and Bombs* by Stephen Barber, but I told him to put a sock in it. My mood was as foul as the weather.

I drove Alan to Netherton, the best-preserved recumbent stone circle in Buchan. I parked just north of the village of Crimond. Like a lot of places we'd been visiting, this ancient monument was on private land but I couldn't be arsed to get the permission of the owner to view it. Since the circle is situated just off the main road between Fraserburgh and Peterhead, I guess a lot of those drawn to it simply trespassed. Both flankers were still standing, as were five other stones. There was a mess of stones inside the circle which might be the remains of a cairn. I lay back against the recumbent. It had stopped raining but the sky was completely overcast and there was very little light.

As Alan came towards me he shimmered, his body was translucent. I thought of the pathless mountains of Iceland, but as the spectre advanced it struck me that the ghosts of the north came from no land known to man or woman. These were the secret people, their kingdom was the north under the *Fir Chlisneach*, the polar aurora. They were always young there. Their bodies were white as the wild swan, their hair yellow as honey, their eyes blue as ice. Their feet left no mark on the snow. The women were white as milk, with eyes like sloes, and lips like red rowans. They fought with shadows and were glad; but the shadows were not shadows to them. The Shee slew great numbers at the full moon; but never hunted on moonless nights, or at the rising of the moon, or when the dew was falling. Their lances were made of reeds that glittered like shafts of ice, and it was ill for a mortal to find one of these lances, for they are tipped with the salt of a wave that no living thing has touched, neither the wailing mew nor the finned *sgádan* nor his tribe, nor the narwhal. There were no men of the human clans there, and no shores, and the tides were forbidden.

As Alan advanced I screamed and my cry was drowned in rolls of thunder and the pealing of lightning. The heavens opened, rain lashed against me and as I lay on that stone altar my legs were forced apart by some unearthly force. Alan pierced me with his lance, then melted into my body and in that terrible downpour the countryside was ruggedly and boldly beautiful, with a sullen suggestion of freedom about it. I thought of my parents and simultaneously banished them from my mind. I'd come to Aberdeenshire to get away from my family. My father had wanted a son and dressed me as a boy until I was twelve. I'd been Anna at school and Alan at home but even after I'd reached puberty Alan would not leave me alone. I'd tried to divorce myself from Alan but what happened at Netherton was better. Alan was melting into me. We were merging just as Old Aberdeen and New Aberdeen, Woodside, Torry and Ruthrieston had been melded into a single city by the sheer force of a growing population. If I could not expel Alan, then I had to gather him up, not to imprison him but to integrate him into my being.

I had to let what was separate exist separately and embrace what remained in all its unity. Aberdeen was quite distinct from the countryside spread before me at Netherton, even if the road north to Ellon and Peterhead was basically an extension of King Street, where I'd once lived. The Don was a natural barrier and the Brig o' Don that had carried me over the river was a marker on my line of flight. The bridge, a fine Gothic arch, was flung over the river, from one rock to the other, the height from the top of the arch to the water is 60 feet, in width 72 feet. It was built by Henry de Cheye, Bishop of Aberdeen, who, on returning to the city after being exiled, applied all the profits that had accumulated during his absence towards the cost of construction. As I looked around me thoughts of water receded, instead I found infinite peace in a frightful disarray of bush and grass, sprinkled with heather and demure bluebells that blushed in the wind and rain. I saw the land as it was, and would be and had been. There was an invoking calm of things past and things to come in dark green woods with arabesque parterres of tinted leaves and mosses with pine needles and pine cones embedded amongst them. Once the skies cleared, the sun would be baffled by the boughs that weaved their shade.

I pictured myself going slowly through the remnant of a forest of old, round about which the woodmen had been terribly busy. Quite suddenly the music of a matchless voice struck my ears, trilling through the listening air like notes from a faultless lute. I stood still and listened. A peasant girl was singing a melodious north-east ballad, for Buchan and Aberdeenshire were the land of the song. It was with the Bronze-Age farmers that the song first invaded what is sometimes called Scotland but might be better understood as south-west Scandinavia. Here the chants of those that had erected the recumbent stone circles were preserved for ages in human hearts, living ever new on human lips, and attuned to undying music and to the strident tones of rushing and falling waters. The history of this part of Scotland, like that of most borderlands, is one of storm and stress; but the raging waters of the North Sea maintained the eastern border of Aberdeenshire intact. Thus the work of the dialectician consists of listening closely to the journeyman and the labourer, since the entire human history of this land is enfolded in the melodious voice of the proletariat. The language of Picts, Celts, Norse, Africans and Saxons is sublated in the Doric.

It is this cultural cross-fertilisation worked through in the common tongue that marks the working class as the progenitors of all the riches of mankind. The voice of the proletariat corrects and redresses the imbalances of bourgeois history, a long-pent-up vigour rushing into expression. It may be melancholy, but it is the matchless, quiet sadness of nature, the deep communion of the mind over which has been thrown for centuries the hypnotic spell of loneliness, the sublimity of silence, the potent lure of quiet places, breeding deep thought untainted by the idealist distortions of bourgeois life. Now that Alan had merged within me his poisoned lance was no longer a threat. I would never meet him again. We would never part. It was only by embracing the gross matter of my body and the wastes it produced that I was able to comprehend my historically determined place in our world.

It was with a sense of wholeness and unity that I trudged alone, but not alone, back to the car. As I made my way through Grimond I picked up a hitch-hiker, who told me his name was Callum and that he was studying geology at Glasgow University. As we talked the shore began to grow bold and rocky, and indented in a strange manner with small and deep creeks, or rather immense and horrible chasms. I suggested we get out of the car and take a walk since no one interested in geology should simply pass by the Bullers of Buchan. This famous landmark is a vast hollow in a rock, projecting into the sea, open at top, with a communication to the sea through a noble natural arch, through which boats can pass, and lie secure in this natural harbour. There is a path round the top, but in some parts so narrow that the traveller must walk hand in hand with fear, as the depth is about 30 fathoms, with water on both sides, being bounded on the north and south with small creeks.

Near this is a great insulated rock, divided by a narrow and very deep chasm from the land. This rock is pierced through midway between the water and the top, and in great storms the waves rush through it with a vast noise and impetuosity. On the sides, as well as those of the adjacent cliffs, breed multitudes of kittiwakes. The young are a local delicacy, being served up a little before dinner, to whet the appetite, but, from the rank smell and taste, seem as if they are more likely to have a contrary effect. I was once told of an honest gentleman who set down for the first time to this appetiser, but after demolishing six with much impatience declared that he had eaten half a dozen and did not find himself a bit more hungry than before he began.

I told Callum we should have sex on the edge of the cliff and then roll ourselves off it if we achieved a simultaneous orgasm. Callum didn't think this was a good idea since it looked like it was coming on to rain again and the ground was already sodden. He proposed we go to my car and make love on the back seat. His suggestion struck me as a typically male fantasy and I scotched it, saying that if we were not going to have sex under the open skies and within earshot of the roaring waves, then we might as well head back to my pad in Aberdeen where we could fuck in comfort. This scenario was quite acceptable to the hitch-hiker, so we returned to the car. Callum attempted to engage me in conversation but his talk bored me, so it was in silence that we drove down King Street, up Union Street and along to Union Grove.

Callum wanted to use the toilet when we got back to the flat. The bulb had gone and I didn't have a spare, so I took the bulb from the light in the hall and transferred it to my windowless bathroom. As my guest relieved himself I stripped. I allowed Callum to take me in his arms and push his roving hand up between my easily separated thighs, where he explored with lecherous fingers the secret charms of my ripe unctuous quim and laid bare the hidden beauties that clustered around the junction of my fleshy thighs. I reclined on the sofa and spread myself open to afford Callum the fullest gratification by a near inspection of the gradually swelling mound and full voluptuous lips of my well-garnished cunt.

While my guest stood over me I unbuttoned his Levi's, pulled up his shirt and drew forth his rod. I took it coaxingly in my well-practised hand and with a stimulating touch passed my fingers gently up and down the shaft and over its pendant head. Then, leaning towards it, I took it into my warm mouth and played around its top and neck with my pliant tongue, while with soft suction I compressed my lips as I moved my head back and forward over it. I played gently with Callum's cock until at last he could no longer stand my soft caresses and plunged his burning tool into my maidenhead. He came quickly taking little care over my pleasure since relief from the boiling tension inside him was the only thing on his mind. After Callum had come I made him tongue my quim so that I too might be afforded respite from the passions that churned within me.

The strip light in the kitchen needed replacing and once it got dark it became impossible to cook. Instead Callum and I wandered up Union Grove to The Déjà Vu. The establishment had recently been converted from a conventional café to a bistro. In the process the prices had doubled. I had tapas, Callum ate a fish dish, we went dutch on the bill. Callum wanted to spend the night at my pad but I told him to dream on and gave him instructions for getting to the youth hostel. Once I hit the sack I dreamt I was a ventriloquist's dummy dreaming I was a woman. I give my dreams as dreams and it is up to the reader to discover whether I reason better when I am asleep, or whether these nightmares are but a fiction and all along the Afro-Celtic social 'body' was wide awake.

ELEVEN

I LET Anna sleep on since she was only hindering my research into K. L. Callan's *69 Things to Do with a Dead Princess*. Besides, I was getting more than a little sick of the conversations she was having with an imaginary friend called Alan. Let me tell you it's no easy thing being a ventriloquist's dummy and the way I was being made to muff-dive every spoilt college girl who got a thrill from molesting inanimate objects was getting on my wick. Anyway, there wasn't much I could do in the house. The sky was overcast and even the light bulb in the toilet had gone. I'd have strained my eyes attempting to read without illumination.

I got into the car. One of Anna's college friends was asleep on the back seat. Nancy woke when I started the engine. She immediately began complaining about the fact that she had an essay to write on *Father and Son* by Edmund Gosse. I sympathised, the book was tiresome. Years ago an English teacher who dabbled in amateur dramatics had attempted to interest a class of thick rich kids in this work by having me discuss it with him. I've always found accounts of childhood in autobiographies inordinately depressing since kids have so little control over their lives. I mentioned *The Grass Arena* by John Healy as an example of this. The early sections of the book, Healy's childhood and time in the army, are tedious. As the book progresses the sense of narrative disintegrates. Instead of a plot Healy offers a series of routines whose random appearance resembles the non-linear structure used by Burroughs for *The Naked Lunch*. Nancy didn't reply or even ask me where we were going. She didn't seem bothered. Not even after we'd passed through Cults and Peterculter. So I just keep talking.

It was a shame that Faber and Faber thought Healy's anti-narrative required a preface from Colin MacCabe. The introduction was quite obviously there for the benefit of middle-brow readers who needed reassurance that in consuming the autobiography of a wino they weren't suffering a lapse of taste. Healy's form suited his descriptions of alcoholic derangement and while his redemption through chess was cheesy in the extreme, once he'd used the game to get off the booze the sudden shift to life on an Indian ashram was a masterfully unsettling stroke. Surreal in much the same way that Bill Drummond's account of a train journey across India in *Annual Report to the Mavericks, Writers and Film Festival* unfolded with the iron logic of a dream. Drummond tearing each page from a book of Ted Hughes poems as he read it, and making these lyrics into paper planes that he threw from a train window.

My conversation flowed and we sped through Banchory to Aboyne. I parked beside the graveyard, pleased that the rain was easing off. We walked up a forest track and found Image Wood stone circle easily enough. It was situated in the trees at the edge of a field. Very close to where a flock of sheep were grazing. There were five stout stones. Three jammed together. Two slightly apart. I didn't think much of the site, although the confusion over whether it was 3000 years old or merely a folly erected in the 18th or 19th century appealed to my sense of the absurd. I took a photograph in which the trunk of a felled tree doubles up as an outlying stone. We left shortly after we'd arrived, having found the site singularly lacking in ambience.

We'd travelled as far west as we were going and I turned east off the service road onto the A93. I retraced the route I'd taken to Aboyne as far as the turn off to Glassel. I parked opposite Glassel House and we walked west along a forest footpath to a burn. The circle was marked on my OS map as being close to the water and somewhere to our south. Locating stones on Forestry Commission land can be a time-consuming business, since it is difficult to orientate oneself by landmarks and the monuments are hidden amongst trees. We walked down a riverside path but after a few minutes we doubled back and worked our way through the trees. There was quite a wind blowing and several pieces of uprooted timber were swaying precariously in the breeze. It took us about five minutes to find the circle. It was in a clearing at the edge of the forest and our goal was illuminated by a burst of sunlight moments after we'd located the stones.

Nancy suggested we have sex and I had to explain that being a ventriloquist's dummy I didn't have a tadger. She said not to worry, then she lay down in the middle of the circle and proceeded to masturbate while I watched. As she adjusted her clothing, Nancy said her orgasm had been extremely intense so she figured the stones must be sited on a very powerful ley line. I told her better was to come since most of the remaining circles I wished to visit that day were recumbents and they'd give her an even bigger thrill. There was a path leading in the direction of the car and it brought us out onto the track we'd taken earlier about 100 yards from where I'd parked. As we sped through Banchory and then onto some back roads at Strachan I mentioned *Memoirs of a Sword Swallower* by Daniel Mannix as an example of an excellent, if obviously unreliable, autobiography.

We talked about Trocchi briefly. Nancy asked me if I'd ever read *The Blue Suit* by Richard Rayner. I'd found both the narrative and the prose tedious in the extreme. Mannered middle-brow bollocks. The skinhead novels that Canadian hack James Moffatt wrote under the name Richard Allen are mentioned twice, and on the second occasion Rayner gets the name wrong and renders it Martin Allen. Besides, even Rayner's literary tastes betrayed him. Hemingway, Camus and Anthony Burgess. The same went for philosophy, where Rayner was given to name-checking Bertrand Russell. An unforgivable sin. Likewise, Rayner's interest in John Aubrey was as a biographer, whereas I knew that Aubrey's *Brief Lives* could have been much improved by being made briefer. Of course, Aubrey could not be ignored but what required confrontation was his work as an antiquarian. It was Aubrey who had first floated the absurd theory that stone circles were Druid temples. It was to be regretted that having engaged James Garden in correspondence about the recumbent circles of Aberdeenshire, Aubrey diverted the theology professor into countering his Druid hobbyhorse at the expense of a detailed description of these mega-lithic sites.

My discourse was interrupted by our arrival at Nine Stanes, also known as Garrol Wood. The site was on Forestry Commission land but, being located very close to the roadside, it is easy to find. We picked our way through the long grass to the stones and sat down on the recumbent. I explained to Nancy that the earlier recumbent circles tended to consist of twelve stones, while later ones such as this contained only nine. We didn't hang about long, since there were still a good many more sites to be visited that day. Doubling back, but only as far as the first turning, we found Esslie the Greater in a boggy field. Just up the road in the next field was Esslie the Lesser, smashed up and overgrown. Our next stop was Cairnfauld, where I parked the car at the top of a muddy farm track. We walked down the lane and since crops were growing in the first field, we cut uphill through the second, which was covered in grass. At the brow of the hill we slipped into a waterlogged and heavily furrowed field, where we were confronted by the stones.

I took one look at the ruined monument and turned around. On our way down the hill Nancy asked me how I'd got interested in stone circles. I decided to use a bit of discretion and made no mention of *69 Things to Do with a Dead Princess*. Instead I bamboozled my companion by mentioning my ongoing research into Lewis Grassic Gibbon's trilogy *A Scots Quair*. When we got back to the car I pulled an omnibus edition of the work from the glove compartment. This was a 1998 edition put out by Penguin for Lomond Books that I'd picked up for a quid in a remainder bookshop. I pointed out the passages I'd highlighted on pages 23, 26, 43, 52, 54, 55, 89, 97, 104, 140, 158, 182, 191, 192, 193, 203, 275, 300 and 332, all of which concerned stone circles. Nancy being Nancy asked me why I'd also highlighted a sentence on page 55 in which a gravestone is described as having a skull and crossbones and an hourglass engraved on it. She became quite indignant when I explained that this was a Masonic grave, claiming that I had no proof!

I started the car and laughed about the blurb on the back of *A Scots Quair*. This claimed that Grassic Gibbon had been compared to Joyce. Unless the comparison was unfavourable it seemed unlikely. The Aberdeenshire scribbler was no modernist and while Joyce was first and foremost a craftsman, the latter's obsession with technique forced him to adopt a progressive world outlook even if he did so without applying conscious thought to the implications of his project. Grassic Gibbon's work was an anachronism, harking back as it did to the output of 19th-century Scots vernacular writers such as William Alexander.[11] Of course, the stones Grassic Gibbon describes as standing beside Blawearie Loch are fictional but they stand in well enough for all the stone circles of Grampian Region. In the course of 'Sunset Song', the first book in Gibbon's trilogy, the stones are initially identified with the Druids, then brought up in a sermon, before being converted into a war memorial. The minister of Gibbon's fictitious Kinraddie even holds a service at the simultaneously old and new war memorial. A symbolic representation of the ongoing desecration of pagan shrines by Christians.

We were speeding south-west on the Slug Road towards Stonehaven at the time I said this to Nancy. I had to admit that 'Sunset Song' was almost competent as a pastiche of the Victorian novel but since the trilogy had been written in the early 1930s there was no way of avoiding the fact that aesthetically it was every bit as reactionary as Gibbon's reprehensible Stalinist politics. 'Cloud Howe' and 'Grey Granite', the other novels that made up the *Scots Quair* trilogy, demonstrated that like all forms of nostalgia Gibbon's literary revisionism operated according to a law of diminishing returns. Likewise, this clown's metaphorical use of the stanes in 'Sunset Song' would have worked far better if he'd avoided erroneously identifying them with the Druids. Since Gibbon wished to document the end of the old agricultural modes of life that began with the Bronze-Age farmers who erected the first standing stones, he'd have done better not to link these monuments with a religion that didn't exist when they were built. Despite being a cornball cliché, the symbolic use of Bennachie as a marker at the end of 'Grey Granite' at least had the merit of being considerably more astute than Gibbon's use of stone circles.

As we got out of the car at the bottom of the lane leading up to West Raedykes farm, I thought it pertinent to mention that Nan Shepherd – another Aberdeenshire author active at the same time as Gibbon – opened her first novel *The Quarry Wood* with Martha Ironside playing on a great cairn of stones. There was a mist where we'd parked and it thickened as we marched up to the farmhouse. The track was muddy and at one point, on a corner where the ground around was absolutely sodden, it had been overlaid with concrete. Lights were on in the farmhouse but we didn't bother knocking at the door to ask permission to go up to the circles beyond it. The fog was getting thicker and you could barely see the farm buildings from halfway up the field behind them. We were still moving up hill and from this point on there were boulders strewn all around us. We examined clumps of bushes and stones and it took us 15 minutes to find the line of ring cairns.

The fog became so thick that it was difficult to see more than a few feet ahead. I had no sense of the landscape in which the stanes stood. I might as well have been looking at an archaeological re-creation in a museum. I told Nancy we should head back down the hill. She said she wanted to look at the Roman fort that lay just across from the stone circles. I told her she was welcome to do so, but I was going back to the car. Nancy saw sense and followed me. Although I had an OS map it didn't do me much good because I couldn't see anything in the fog. I kept silent about the fact that I'd left my compass in the car and strode off in what I hoped was the right direction, with Nancy struggling to keep up. My bearings were off and I corrected them when I spotted a couple of poles to my right which had been that side of us on our way up. Having got down to the farmhouse, it was simply a matter of following the lane until we reached my Fiesta.

Once I'd caught my breath I drove to the Slug Road, then headed south-west towards Stonehaven before swinging north up the A90. Just before Portlethen I took a left and rode the back roads, parking at the top of a lane that led down to a stud farm. We trotted along the farm track and cut across a field. There were two stone circles, Auchquhorthies and Old Bourtreebush close by each other and lying just five miles south of Aberdeen. One of them had two circles of stones, whereof the exterior circle consists of 13 great stones, besides two that are fallen and a broad stone towards the south about three yards high above the ground, the uprights stand between seven and eight paces distant from each other. The diameter is 24 large paces, the interior circle is about eight paces distant from the outer, and the stones of the smaller circle stand about three feet above the ground. Towards the east from this monument at 26 paces distance, there is a big stone fast in the ground and level with it, in which there is a cavity partly natural and partly artificial, that will contain, as I guess, no less than a Scotch gallon of water, and may be supposed to have served for washing the priests, sacrifices and other things esteemed sacred among the heathens.

Old Bourtreebush stone circle is fully as large and lies about a bowshot distant from Auchquhorthies. It consists of three circles with a common centre. The stones of the greatest circle are about eight feet and those of the two lesser circles about three feet above ground, the innermost circle is three paces in diameter and its stones stand close together. One of the stones of the outer circle on the west side of the monument has a cavity in its top, considerably lower at one side, which could contain an English pint without running over. Another stone of the same circle on the east side has at its top a narrow cavity about three fingers deep, into which is cut a trough one inch thick and two inches broad, with another of the same depth crossing it and runs down the length of the stone a good way. Nancy suggested that we have sex in the circle but once I'd reminded her that I didn't have a wanger she walked dejectedly back to the car.

We cut up towards the Dee and, remaining south of this river, visited Clune Hill stone circle, another beautiful recumbent. We parked at a forest gate and a couple of posh girls out riding on their ponies greeted us as we stalked up the hill. Nothing worthy of commemoration took place during this visit or those to various other sites around Insch and Alford. We took in Kinellar Kirk and gazed at the stone in the kirkyard wall that had once been part of a circle now destroyed and replaced by a church. I talked about Oxford and its corrupting influence. One only had to look at a novelist like Simon Mason, who'd been a student at Lady Margaret Hall and gone on to work at the Varsity Press, to know that Oxford must be condemned. Mason's father might have been a professional footballer but one would never have guessed it from the odious descriptions of Oxford in his mediocre second novel *Death of a Fantasist*.

After visiting Tyrebagger Hill we took a wander around the airport and Dyce village. The parish of Dyce lies from five to eight miles north-west of Aberdeen. The origin of its name is unknown. It is bounded by Newhills on the south and south-west, Kinellar on the north-west, Fintray on the north, New Machar and Old Machar on the east. Its length is about six miles, its greatest breadth about three miles. The figure of the parish is nearly oval, slightly curved at the narrower extremity, and lying from north-west to south-east. The north-west, or broader, end of the oval is formed by a low hill called Tyrebagger, which extends downwards to the south-east nearly three miles, or half the extreme length of the parish, after which, rapidly descending, it merges with the adjacent plains.

Rather than talking to Nancy of geology or zoology, I said that although there were a handful of brilliant English novelists such as the London-based Welshman Iain Sinclair, overall Americans showed a greater aptitude for sculpting our shared language into fresh forms. Nancy told me to shut up, she was bored with my conversation and said that if I couldn't fuck her, she wanted to murder me. I had to explain that being a ventriloquist's dummy I was inanimate and that therefore I couldn't be killed. Nancy rejoined that she might not be able to slay me but she could, at least, give it her best shot. My companion took a gun from her pocket and ordered me back to the car. I was made to open the boot and get into it. I found myself trapped in darkness and thinking of Jennifer Lopez in the film *Out of Sight*. Actually, I wasn't so much thinking about Jennifer Lopez as about a specific part of her anatomy. To be more precise I was thinking about her bottom. It was enormous and I didn't so much like the shots of George Clooney touching it once he'd got Lopez trapped in the trunk of a car, as those scenes after Jennifer was injured when she had on a pair of sports shorts. The film itself was quite forgettable, one of those dot-to-dot crime thrillers adapted from a crummy Elmore Leonard novel. But Jennifer Lopez's bottom was something else. Art and nature hadn't combined to produce such pleasing results since the hosing-down sequence at the beginning of the Pamela Anderson vehicle *Barb Wire*. There isn't much to do when you're stuck in the boot of a car, which I guess is why my thoughts were wandering.

Eventually the car pulled up and when Nancy opened the boot I realised we were at Sunhoney. With a gun at my back Nancy marched me up past the farmhouse to the stone circle. When we stopped she told me to take my pants down. Perhaps I thought breathlessly, Nancy hadn't believed me when I'd told her I was wadgerless and everything would

be okay once she realised I hadn't lied. Although I'm only a
ventriloquist's dummy, if I were a man I'd be a red-blooded
male with a taste for hefty strawberry-blondes like Nancy.
It wasn't that I didn't find Nancy attractive but when I
looked down to where I should have had an erection, there
was nothing there. The only things hanging down from
the lower parts of my body were my legs. Nancy laughed
cruelly and called me a nothing man. Then she told me to
take off the rest of my clothes. After this, Nancy nailed me
by my hands to one of the many trees that surrounded the
stone circle.

Sunhoney stone circle is beautifully set on a low knoll that
is fringed by a ring of trees. It is surrounded on all sides by
taller hills that echo its spherical shape. Most of the stones
were still standing but the heavily cup-marked recumbent
had fallen forward into the circle. Nancy lay back on this
great slab of granite and, hitching up her skirt, worked
her fingers under the waistband of her white knickers. She
stared up at me nailed to the tree as she worked herself
into a frenzy, threshing about on that great slab of stone. I
didn't know where to look. I tried focusing on some of the
uprights but they seemed so phallic that I shifted my gaze
to the ring cairn in the centre of the circle. Unfortunately
this feature was quite ruined and hard to make out. Finally
I found myself ogling Nancy. She really was magnificent. A
big girl with her long red hair splayed behind her shoulders
and a hand down her panties. At that moment I deeply
regretted the fact that I didn't have a dick. Although I
was the symbolic equivalent of a supine recumbent I found
myself identifying with the phallic flankers.

Once Nancy finished pleasuring herself and had adjusted
various pieces of clothing, she took me down from the tree
and forced me back into the boot of the car. It was pitch-
black and, with nothing to see or do, I found my thoughts

returning to Jennifer Lopez's bottom. I can picture it now, graceful and round, the buttocks filling out her shorts to perfection. When the car stopped and the boot was opened, it was dark outside. It wasn't until we'd got down to the lake that I realised Nancy had driven me to Loch Skene, the largest single expanse of fresh water in Aberdeenshire. The moon appeared from behind a cloud and the lake was bathed in an eerie glow. Nancy made me stand at the edge of the loch and put the gun to my head. The retort after she pulled the trigger was quite deafening and the bullet buried itself harmlessly in the stuffing that would have been my brains had I not been inanimate.

Nancy stamped her foot in anger and I laughed. I stopped laughing when she ordered me to get into the water. I protested that I couldn't swim but Nancy insisted that she already knew this. With the gun trained upon me I waded further and further out into the cool water. I must have been walking on a shelf because suddenly there was nothing beneath my feet and I found myself falling through endless fathoms. Eventually I hit some submerged rocks, from where I could see a wreck resting at the bottom of the loch, amidst the weeds. The ship had all three of her lower masts in, and her lower yards squared. But what caught my eye more than anything else was a great superstructure, which had been built upwards from the rails, almost halfway to the main tops, and this, as I was able to perceive, was supported by ropes let down from the yards. Of what material the superstructure was composed I have no knowledge, for it was so overgrown with weeds – as was as much of the hull that could be seen amidst the luxurious growth of freshwater plants – as to defy my guesses. And because of the growth it came to me that the ship must have been lost to the world a very great time ago. At this realisation I grew full of solemn thoughts, and not even once did I think of Jennifer Lopez's

well-padded arse, for it seemed to me that I had come upon
the cemetery of Loch Skene.

As I was too exhausted from the day's excitements to
make my way towards the strange vessel, I just lay where I'd
come to rest at the bottom of the loch, falling presently into
a deep sleep. In my slumbers I dreamt that I was a woman
dreaming I was a ventriloquist's dummy. I give my dreams
as dreams and I hope it is as dreams that other dreamers
will receive them. Hallucinations within the hallucination
that was already speech.

TWELVE

I AWOKE screaming. My cries echoed around the empty room. I'd sold my books, most of the furniture, there wasn't even a working light bulb in the flat. I got up from the bare mattress I'd slept upon, slipped into the only jumper and pair of jeans I had. There was nothing to eat in the fridge, in fact there wasn't even a fridge. I'd flogged it a few days earlier. There wasn't time to eat in a café, I had an appointment with my tutor. I went out to the car. Someone had broken into it. The side window was smashed, my ventriloquist's dummy had been stolen. I put my bad dreams down to some psychic alarm that had been triggered by the theft. I cleared the broken glass from the passenger seat, then dived into the Bungalow Shoppe to buy a Mars bar before driving to the university.

My tutor was worried about me. He said I was bright but insisted I was going off the rails. He described my essays as brilliant and with a flourish of his hand emphasised that this didn't entitle me to skip lectures. The professor had called my family and learnt I was estranged from them. He'd discovered I hadn't seen my parents for more than a year and that they were unwilling to visit me unless they received an invitation. My mother had called on me unannounced shortly after I'd started my degree and I'd slammed the front door of my flat in her face. I hadn't spoken to her since. Since my parents were unwilling to

visit, a compromise had been suggested. A friend of my
father's was now living in Aberdeen, my tutor gave me
his phone number. I was reluctant to call him but the
professor made it clear he expected me to meet up with
this man if the matter of my poor attendance was to be
overlooked. He'd also booked me an appointment with the
college psychologist. I hated shrinks, I'd been sent to several
before I left home. They all seemed to think that my sex life
was something I ought to share with them. Dirty old men.

We discussed my dissertation. I wanted to read *Camden
Girls* by Jane Owen, through *On The Road* and *Ulysses*.
Camden Girls utilised a taken-for-granted model of bourgeois subjectivity, so this would give me the opportunity to
address the recuperation of both high modernism and trash
by the culture industry. Owen used present-tense stream-
of-consciousness to recreate in novel form the concerns
of mass-circulation women's magazines. It didn't really
matter whether or not Owen had read Joyce, because
even if she had her consumption of him was obviously
filtered through pop culture. Owen had never encountered
Joyce in all his originality, nor understood the nature of his
break with naturalism and the bourgeois subject. When my
tutor attempted to interrupt this speech I told him to forget
about Henry Miller.

I wanted to situate Owen in the context of both Brit
pop and Brit art. There were incredible parallels between
Camden Girls and 90s art. A recycling of conceptual-
ism which stripped away the political content of its 60s
model and replaced this with vapid pop-cultural referents.
Popular literature was also a useful sounding board. Read
ahistorically, Owen and Kerouac were male and female mir-
ror images of each other. However, for all their weaknesses,
Kerouac's texts were enriched by the tension created from
his resistance to the dominant literary styles of 50s America.

The same could not be said for Owen. *Camden Girls* does not resist the reader. Rather than offering a critique of commodification, Owen celebrates capital for its ability to homogenise the vast plurality of world cultures, stripping them of every trace of their social origin before offering them up in sanitised form for consumption by white bourgeois subjects. Books such as *Camden Girls* always stress the middle-class identity of their central characters.

My tutor wasn't very impressed by these ideas. He pulled a few books off a shelf, all women writers. *Insanity* by Anna Reynolds, *Debatable Land* by Candia McWilliam, *The Rest of Life* by Mary Gordon. I was told to go away and look at these works, they were more literary, would make better subjects for my dissertation if I really insisted on doing contemporary fiction. I left, put the car in a garage to have the window repaired, phoned my father's friend Callum and arranged to meet him in The Grill. I was early, Callum was late. I leafed through the books I'd been given. McWilliam didn't appeal at all, she was born in Edinburgh and the professor seemed over-keen to get me to read Scottish fiction. Mary Gordon was more compelling than Anna Reynolds. America triumphing yet again over England. The covers of all three books made them look like remainders, the Anna Reynolds design being the most extraordinary. A girl in a black sleeveless dress with her head thrown back, dark red curtains behind her, a perfect cliché. However, the typography was truly shocking, the letter 'A' being bigger and thicker than the same sized 'S' and 'N', which were bigger than the first 'N' and second 'I', which were bigger than the first 'I' and 'Y'. The letters were like a series of steps, up and down. Down and up. Back and forth. Round and round. Ghastly. Ugly. My eyes took in the type but it became jumbled in my brain. It made me feel sick. I wobbled across the bar. Ordered another gin.

Callum arrived. He bought me a drink. Gin and it. He got himself a pint of heavy. He was younger than I expected. Mid-30s. He'd worked with my father until a new and better job brought him to the north-east. Callum had an English accent. He explained that he'd been born in London but his family was Scottish, hence his name. He asked me how I was getting along at college. I laughed, then fell silent. Callum said he'd let me into a secret if I promised not to tell my dad. I agreed after pointing out that the promise was superfluous since I wasn't speaking to my parents. Callum said he'd been sacked from his job. He'd been caught stealing a computer and some cash. He was surviving on his savings. He told me that he found my dad very conservative, that my family weren't friends, merely acquaintances. I decided that I liked Callum, so I took him back to my flat. He was shocked to see how empty it was, said we'd be more comfortable at his place on King Street. We went. His flat was stuffed with books.

Callum asked me if I knew anything about the writer Andrew Sinclair. My reply was negative. Callum didn't much like Sinclair's best-selling first novel *The Breaking of Bumbo*, but candidly admitted the prose was both more free-form and free-flowing than in the follow-up *My Friend Judas*. Sinclair was part of the Angry Young Man syndrome and thus just a big yawn as far as Callum was concerned. A slight semi-autobiographical novel about being in the Guards and an even slighter follow-up about undergraduate life in Cambridge quickly and quietly transformed Sinclair into a forgotten old man of English letters.

Sinclair, if his autobiography *In Love and Anger* was to be believed, had been in all the right places at all the right times. He'd been with the Black Panthers in Cuba. It was merely unfortunate that being an establishment man he had nothing interesting to say about this. *The Last of the Best:*

The Aristocracy of Europe in the Twentieth Century shows Sinclair at his most controversial, where with a delicate sense of irony he suggests that toffs should bring elegance to their passing as they fade from the ranks of the living and into the realm of history. *The Need to Give: The Patrons and the Arts* was equally turgid if somewhat wider in its historical scope. In this work Sinclair gave art collectors like Charles Saatchi his endorsement. The men he praised had little need of such support. Perhaps Sinclair thought these men were supporting him. By the early 90s Sinclair could still command decent advances even if most of his books were almost instantly remaindered.

In *The Sword and the Grail* Sinclair rehashed a vast amount of historical material about the Templars and the fact that he is a direct descendant of Prince Henry St Clair was used to boost his flagging credibility. Unfortunately for Sinclair he wasn't quite as credulous as most of those who write popular works about monastic military orders and secret societies. Sinclair saw Rosslyn Chapel as being the real treasure of the Templars, not exactly the most sensational of conclusions. That said, *The Sword and the Grail* appeared to have been Sinclair's most popular book since *The Red and the Blue: Intelligence, Treason and the Universities.* According to Callum, Sinclair's choice of subjects wasn't nearly as wide-ranging as they at first appeared. From the Cambridge Apostles, who'd refused to admit Sinclair into their ranks, to the key role of Sinclair's ancestors in the affairs of the Knights Templar was a very short step. If Sinclair didn't write well, he was at least consistent in writing about himself regardless of whether the result was marketed as fiction or a historical study.

I asked Callum what he'd been doing since he'd stopped working. He said he was researching recumbent stone circles.

He wanted to get a fresh insight into the profusion of mega-lithic remains scattered across Aberdeenshire. Most people visited clusters of circles, slowly working their way around the different parts of Grampian Region. Callum was visiting them alphabetically by name. That way he was getting to see the stanes in a totally fresh light. He showed me a list of sites he'd compiled: Aikey Brae, Ardlair, Arnhill, Auchlee, Auchmachar, Auchmaliddie, Auchquhorthies, Auld Kirk o' Tough, Backhill of Drachlaw East and West, Balhalgardy, Balnacraig, Balquhain, Bellman's Wood, Berrybrae, Bing-hill, Blue Cairn, Bogton Lhanbryde, Bourtreebush aka Old Bourtreebush, Braehead Leslie, Brandsbutt Inverurie, Broomend of Auchleven, Broomed of Crichie aka Druids-field, Cairnborrow Gingomyres, Cairnfauld, Cairnhall, Cairn-ton, Cairnwell, Camp, Candle Hill of Ardoyne aka Hatton of Ardoyne, Candle Hill of Insch, Candle Hill of Rayne aka Old Rayne, Candy, Carlin Stone aka Cairn Riv, Castle Fraser, Chapel o' Sink and Ark Stone, Clune Hill aka Raes of Clune, Corrie Cairn, Corrstone Wood, Corrydoun, Cortes, Cothiemuir Wood, Craighead, Crookmuir, Cullerlie aka Standing Stones of Echt, Culsalmond, Culsh, Currachs, Deer Park Monnymusk, Doune of Dalmore, Druidsfield, Druidstone, Drumfours Cushnie, Dunnydeer, Dunnydeer North, East Crichie, Easter Aquhorthies, Easter Fornet at Skene, Esslie the Greater, Esslie the Lesser, Forvie Sands, Frendraught, Fullerton, Gask aka Springhill, Gaul Cross, Gaval, Gavenie Braes, Gingomyres, Glassel, Gowk Stane, Gray Stane, Gray Stane Clochforbie, Greystone aka Auld Kirk, Hare Stanes and Woof Stane, Hillhead Bankhead of Clatt, Hill of Fiddes, Huntly, Image Wood, Inchmarlow, Innesmill Urquhart, Inschfield, Jericho-Colpy, Kinellar Kirk, Kirkton of Bourtie, Langstane o' Aberdeen, Langstane o' Craigearn, Leys of Dummuie, Loanend aka Hawkhill, Loanhead of Daviot, Loudon Wood, Mains of

Hatton, Marionburgh, Marnoch Kirk and Bellman Wood, Melgum, Midmar and Balblair, Mill of Carden, Millplough, Mundurno, Nether Balfour aka Whitefield, Nether Corskie, Nether Coullie, Nether Dumeath, Netherton, New Craig, Nine Stanes (Mulloch) aka Garrol Wood, North Burreldales, North Strone, Old Keig, Old Wester Echt, Peathill, Pinkie Stanes, Pitglassie, Raedykes, Raich, Rothiemay, St Brandan's Stanes, Sandend, Sheldon, Shethin aka Raxton, Skellmuir Hill, South Fornet, South Leylodge and Leylodge Fetter-letter complexes, South Ythsie, Standing Stanes o' Strath-bogie, Stonehead, Strichen, Sunhoney, Sunken Kirk aka Tofthills of Clatt, Tamnagorn, Templand aka Upper Ord, Templestone, Temple Stones, Thorax, Tilquhillie, Tom-naverie, Tuach, Tyrebagger, Upper Auchnagorth, Upper Crichie, Upper Lagmore, Upper Third, Wantonwells, Waulkmill, Wells of Ythan aka Logie Newton, Wheedle-mont aka Cailleach, White Cow Wood, Whitehill Wood, White Lady of Tillyfoure aka Whitehill, Witches' Stones, Yonder Bognie and Westerton

I asked Callum how he had arrived at an alphabetical order for the circles when there were both variant spellings and variant names. He said it didn't matter. How random is random? Where there'd been choices he'd opted for the name or spelling that most appealed to him. There was no definitive list of Grampian stone circles. Of course, many of the circles Callum listed had been destroyed but we could still visit the sites and imagine what was, or at least what might have been. Callum asked me if I'd like to accompany him to the Auld Kirk o' Tough since he was going there that afternoon. I agreed but insisted we took a walk on the beach before leaving. On the way out of the flat I noticed several unopened letters addressed to Alan MacDonald.

We strode down to the seafront. White foam, gulls whirling above our heads. Down on the beach we couldn't see the cafés or the esplanade that ran from them to the western edge of the sea defences. The smell of salt. Seaweed that was salt encrusted. The ocean vast, heaving, amorphous. The white surf, lights of ships bobbing on the waves. White spray, surf, the roar of water forever rising and falling. I pressed a palm against my forehead. I felt all at sea. No longer knew who I was, whether anything separated me from that great mass of work. The ocean, the desert, inside outside, all around. What was I doing? I had to get away from the water. My mind spinning. I was in danger of falling. I mumbled something to Callum.

We turned around, turned back to the beginning, climbed up onto the esplanade. There was no beginning. Saw that cars were still cruising up and down the strip. The mystery was resolved with the stroke of a pen. We'd stopped living. The beginning did not, could not, exist prior to the end. A man no longer called Alan came to Aberdeen. He told me his name was Callum. I believed him. Interpretation spelt out the elements of a dream. Hallucinations within the hallucination that was already speech. The body of a dead princess as a metaphor for literature. Works of condensation and displacement. Living out the death of these fantasies in blasted and blistered night, we were consumed by the turning of a page . . .[12]

FOOTNOTES

1. How different this 'seaside' town is to Ann Quin's imaginary! The prose in this opening section and at the close splits the difference between Gertrude Stein and Samuel Beckett. Avoiding Ernest Hemingway, I detour instead towards Ann Quin. Disliking Hemingway, I detour instead towards Ann Quin. Avoiding Stein, I detour instead towards Ann Quin. Disliking Stein, I detour instead towards Ann Quin. Feeling Beckett is too obvious a point of reference, I detour instead towards Ann Quin. Despite ongoing rumours of a B. S. Johnson revival, I feel our attention could be more usefully directed towards Ann Quin.

2. Alan's sexual prowess is arresting because British Intelligence are after him for pandering and plagiarism. Alan also got into trouble recently for calling Julian Barnes 'effeminate'. After much argument he managed to convince a number of his drinking cronies that by 'effeminate' he meant 'someone who literary reviewers often profile as an English experimental novelist he ha'. Incidentally, Alan's principal difficulty is that he has been unsuccessful in getting his fellow pissheads to call him 'Callum' – something they refuse to do because of the alarming frequency with which he makes anonymous heavy-breather calls and the fact that he insists on drinking expensive malts like Springbank and Talisker.

3. In *A Thousand Plateaus* Deleuze and Guattari usefully theorise microfascism as a phenomenon that exists across the

political and social spectrum. Nevertheless, despite reiterating Jean-Pierre Faye's description of the cry 'Long live death!' as stupid and repugnant, D & G fail to address how this slogan functions or indeed why it is so well suited to the necessarily ambiguous agenda of fascist modernism. As well as celebrating destruction, 'Long live death!' simultaneously announces the death of death and the birth of a new and supposedly 'immortal' order. If D & G attacked the implied rhetorical claim that 'Death is dead, long live death!', there would be little need to read Norman O. Brown's *Life against Death* as a counterbalance to the faulty logic of their over-rationalised 'reasoning'. D & G simply don't understand that the slogan 'Long live death!' sets up an irresolvable dynamic between opposed but balanced meanings. There is an aphorism traditionally attributed to the poet Jeppe Aakjaer that will usefully assist us in reorienting this debate: 'I learn nothing from the dead words of living men. I learn everything from the living words of dead men – long live the dead.' Obviously, Baudrillard's *Symbolic Exchange and Death* provides another line of flight within this debate. For a critique of Baudrillard's positions on death see 'The Margins Of Theosophy' by Stewart Home in *Re: Action 9* (London, Autumn Equinox 399 MKE).

While it goes without saying that D & G's theorisation of desire as productive is useful in undermining the notion of repression and thus the entire edifice of organised psychoanalysis, their concept of the machinic production of desire is still grounded in a massive and unexamined belief in the so-called unconscious. Likewise, in reading Brown on death against D & G, it is also necessary to read D & G on becoming animal against Brown. D & G's pack machine should be hooked up to Brown's individuality machine. Likewise, D & G's anti-Hegelian rhetoric machine must be hooked up to the many master/slave dialectic machines that have already attached themselves to Brown's reading of Hegel in his chapters on death. Despite D & G's attacks on Hegel as a State philosopher, there are readings of Hegel that when hooked up to D & G's anti-Oedipal machine greatly strengthen their analysis of microfascism. With regard to this Paul Gilroy's interpretation of the master/slave dialectic in *The Black Atlantic: Modernity and Double Consciousness* is crucial. Likewise, *Judaism and Modernity: Philosophical Essays* by Gillian Rose is a useful point of reference for those negotiating Gilroy's œuvre. We must be careful not to over-rationalise capitalist societies since it was precisely this error that led to the sorry spectacle of 'ultra-left' negationism.

4. Payne's experiences can be usefully contrasted with the urban myth about a mental patient who was subjected to a lie-detector test in which he was asked if he was the writer Kathy Acker. Guessing correctly that the doctors wanted him to deny his 'true' identity, the patient told the two men interrogating him what they hoped to hear. However, the lie detector indicated he was lying. This fanatical belief in their own bullshit is doubly true of unsuccessful writers named Joseph Farquharson, a dead Aberdeenshire painter famous for his rustic scenes featuring sheep and snow.

5. As well as disliking Raymond Queneau's fiction and the dandyism implicit in it, I also feel extremely ambivalent about his role in assembling Alexandre Kojève's talks on Hegel. While it is useful to have access to Kojève's lectures, I nevertheless believe that, by bringing them to print, Queneau extended their already deleterious impact on French culture. Kojève's simplistic reading of Hegel quickly became a standard one among Marxist intellectuals in post-war France.

6. I shit you not and let me assure you that after eating this Clatterin Brig Restaurant house speciality, I made good use of the toilets located between the dining area and the gift shop. It should, however, go without saying that this

platter is a big improvement on Blaster Al Ackerman's clam-supreme surprise which surprises all of those who eat it when they discover they've caught botulism. After visiting Ackerman in Baltimore and consuming the fare he offered me, I went around for several days thinking I was a ventriloquist's dummy and going 'toot toot'. Unfortunately, I'm not sure whether it was the 'vegetarian' clam-supreme surprise he made in my honour or the Four Roses bourbon we drank that had the more noxious effect.

7. On top of being stupid, Jay Allan is every inch the privileged bigot facetiously placing the blame for racism on its victims. For example, he rants about there being football troubles 'wherever there is a drop of Irish blood thick enough to recall 1690'.

8. I also recorded another dream from that night in my diary. In the earlier dream I dreamt I was my future husband Dudley Standing and that we'd been married for 15 years. Our relationship had long ago reached that stage known among Fleet Street hacks as 'married patience'. My spiralling overdraft provided conclusive proof that like my love life, my career was in terminal decline. The bottom had dropped out of the market for my brand of underground movie-making, which was basically soft-porn dressed up as art. For reasons that had always remained obscure to me, there was a time when millions of university-educated men would only watch an actress get her kit off if she mumbled a few lines paraphrased from an existentialist philosopher before indulging in nude frolics. The craze for amateur porn, which many intellectuals view as 'non-exploitative', thanks to the participants' supposedly eager and unpaid engagement in sexual athletics, had put me out of business.

My financial worries manifested themselves physically, much to Anna's chagrin, and for more than two years, I'd been unable to get it up. However, the lack of physical intimacy between us was the least of our worries. Thanks to negative equity, it wasn't possible to take out a second mortgage on our home, and it looked increasingly likely that our eldest son would have to give up his public-school education, due to my inability to cover the fees. I suppose Anna has always worn the trousers in our relationship, and it was her bright idea that I should try my hand at faking amateur porn, which, with its ultra-low budgets, is highly lucrative. The wife even suggested that we could star in our own production. My immediate response was that this was an absurd idea because at the time I was incapable of doing anything more hard-core than a nude kiss and cuddle. Anna, ever the practical mind, pointed out that this was not really a problem, because we could contact men looking for a free shag through the classified advertisement sections carried by the less reputable type of glamour magazine. All that would be required of me was the ability to point a camera lens at extended bouts of horizontal action.

Leafing through various girlie rags, I was dismayed by the crudity of tone employed by many of those seeking their jollies in the sexual underground. Messages along the lines of 'you can screw my missus if you don't mind me watching' were obviously phrased to attract the attention of building labourers and other undesirable types. Since Anna was sacrificing herself for the good of our family, I wanted to track down some caring and sensitive men. My first attempt at a classified – written in Latin with several very witty classical allusions – met with no response whatsoever. Eventually I placed an ad that stated: 'Ornithologist with own bird seeks males to interact with his pet. Photo essential, video audition awaits. Here's looking at you, kid!' While those involved in the sexual fringe seem to thrive on its seediness, I hoped that by very partially veiling my desire to engage in voyeurism I would discourage the more extreme brand of degenerate.

The first contact we invited to our house described himself as a book collector. Alan seemed a pleasant enough chap, he chatted about contemporary classical music over several cups of tea until Anna suggested we all make our way up to the bedroom. Alan's character underwent a drastic change the moment he spotted the oversized tailor's dummy that had been used in one of my films and was subsequently kept as a memento of a highly successful shoot. Alan immediately leapt at the mannequin, wrestling it to the floor, all the while screaming: 'Help me, Jennifer, help help me Jennifer.' Anna rushed to the phone and called the police while I barricaded myself and the children into an upstairs bedroom.

This defensive reflex proved unnecessary because Alan attempted to crawl into the dummy, all the while relating how the highlight of his life was an unpleasant scene he'd created early one morning in Charing Cross Station. The cad boasted of upsetting a party of schoolgirls by spilling what he called his 'genetic wealth' into a basket filled with skinhead gear, old pieces of laundry, dead peafowls and artificial limbs, while dressed in a pillow-case hood and claiming to be called 'Young Ling'. It turned out that our guest was well known to the local health authority and he was eventually carried from the house in a straitjacket, bellowing, 'Come, feel my love muscle,' at the top of his voice. This incident had a number of unpleasant repercussions, not the least of which was the fact that several of our neighbours stopped speaking to us.

9. Alan never did present me with a copy of his bibliography. Among his papers that I now possess is a page that might be a sketch for this missing document. It runs as follows: 'BOOKS/PAPERS. Refer to Burl, Hayman, Garden, Gordon, James Anderson 1779, Pennant 1774, Society of Antiquaries of Scotland, *Archaeology and Prehistoric Annals of Scotland* by Wilson 1851, *Sculptured Stones of Scotland* by

J. Stuart 1856, *Rude Stone Monuments in All Countries* by
Ferguson 1872, *Hill Forts* . . . and *What Mean These Stones*
by MacLagan 1875 and 1894, *Broomend of Crichie* PSAS by
Dalrymple 1884, *Stone Circles near Aberdeen* JRAI by Lewis
1888, Fred Coles 1899–1910, Norman Lockyer, Rev. Browne,
Sir A Ogston, Pixley, Campbell, Foster Forbes, Watkins.'

From this bald page and my own researches in the reference section of Aberdeen Library I have constructed a
bibliography that I believe comes close to replicating Alan's
missing work. It goes like this:

Aberdeen Spalding Club (1843) *Collection for a History of the
Shires of Aberdeen and Banff*
Aberdeen Spalding Club (1847–69) *Antiquities of the Shires of
Aberdeen and Banff*
Alexander, W. M. (1952) *Place Names of Aberdeenshire* Aberdeen
Ashmore, P. J. (fthcomng) *Temples and Tombs* London: Batsford
Boece, Hector (1527) *History of Scotland*
Browne, Rev. G. F. (1921) *On some Antiquities in the Neighbour-
hood of Dunnecht house, Aberdeenshire* Cambridge 7700.f.12
Brown, P. L. (1979) *Megalithic Masterminds* (Robert Hale,
London)
Burl, A. (1979) *Rings of Stone: Prehistoric Stone Circles of Britain
and Ireland* Frances Lincoln Publishers Ltd x.322/8945
Burl, H. A. W. (1976) *Stone Circles of the British Isles* Yale
X.421/10279 WW
Garden, J. (1766) *A Copy of a Letter from the Rev. James
Garden . . . to John Aubrey* (1692) *Archaeologia*
Gordon, Cosmo A. (ed.) (1960) *Letters to John Aubrey* Miscel-
lany of the Third Spalding Club (Aberdeen)
Feachem, R. (1963) *A guide to Prehistoric Scotland* Batsford
7711.t.39
Forbes, J. F. (1945) *Giants of Britain* (Thomas' Publications) 7711
a.21 St Pan

Forbes, J. F. (1948) *The Castle and Place of Rothiemay* 7822 bbb 35 St Pan

Forbes, J. F. *Living Stones of Britain* WP 8387 WW

Grinsell, L. V. (1976) *Folklore of Pre-historic Sites in Britain* Newton Abbot

Hannah, I.C. (1934) *The Story of Scotland in Stone* Oliver and Boyd 07815.eee.54

Hayman, R. (1997) *Riddles in Stone: Myths, Archaeology and the Ancient Britons* YC.1997.b.839

Heggie, H. (1981) *Megalithic Science* London

Keiller, A. (1934) *The Megalithic Monuments of North East Scotland* A reprint for the Morven Institute of Archaeological Research, London

Kirk, W. (1953) *Prehistoric Sites at the Sands of Forvie, Aberdeenshire* Aberdeen

Lewis, A.L. (1888) *Some Stone Circles near Aberdeen Journal of the Royal Anthropological Institute (JRAI)* 17 pp44–57

Lockyer, J. (1906) *Stonehenge and Other British Stone Monuments Astronomically Considered* London 07709.cc.8

MacDonald, J. (1900) *Place Names of West Aberdeenshire* Ac.1483

MacDonald, J. (1891) *Place Names in Strathbogie* Spalding Club 12978.c.34

MacKenzie, D. A. (1930) *Scotland: The Ancient Kingdom* 9510.bb.13

MacKenzie, D. A. (1935) *Scottish Folklore and Folklife* 20018.g.31

Mackie, E. (1977) *Science and Society in Prehistoric Britain* London

MacLagan, C. (1875) *Hill Forts, Stone Circles . . . of Ancient Scotland* Edinburgh 7708g3

MacLagan, C. (1894) *What Mean these Stones?* Edinburgh 07708.g.35

McPherson, J. M. (1929) *Primitive Beliefs in the North East of Scotland* Longmans 010006.f.35

Miller, H. (1834–1902) *Scenes and Legends of the North of Scotland* Edinburgh?

Ogston, Sir A. (1931) *The Prehistoric Antiquities of the Howe of Cromar* Aberdeen, Third Spalding Club Ac.8246(2)

Pennant, T. (1774) *A Tour in Scotland* 3rd Edition, Warrington 567.c.2

Piggot, S. (ed.) (1962) *The Prehistoric Peoples of Scotland* London W.P.D. 397/5

Ritchie, A. (1989) *Scotland BC* Edinburgh

Ritchie, G. and A. (1981) *Scotland: Archaeology and Early History* London

Ruggles, C. L. N. & Clive (1984) *Megalithic Astronomy . . . Study of 300 Western Scottish Sites* x.425/5449

Ruggles, C. L. N. & Burl, A. (1985) *A New Study of the Aberdeenshire Recumbent Stone circles, 2. Interpretation* in *Journal for the History of Astronomy* (JHA) 8, S27–S60 (Journal also referred to as *Archaeoastronomy*)

Shepherd, I. A. G. (1986) *Exploring Scotland's Heritage: Grampian* Edinburgh BS. 170/14

Shepherd, I. A. G. (1996) *Aberdeen and North East Scotland* HMSO BS.170/30

Shepherd, I. A. G. (1987) *The Early Peoples* in Omand, D (ed) *The Grampian Book* Golspie YC.1989.a.5763

Scott-Moncrieff, G. *The Stones of Scotland* Batsford

Simpson, W. D. *The Ancient Stones of Scotland* Hale X410/300 (1944) *The Province of Mar* AU Studies no. 121

Stuart, J. (1856) *Sculptured Stones of Scotland* AC.8244/17

Thom, A. (1967) *Megalithic Sites in Britain* Oxford: Clarendon x.410/720

Thom, A. *Megalithic Lunar Observations* x620/1857

Thom, Thom & Burl (1980) *Megalithic Rings: Plans and Data for 229 monuments in Britain* Oxford

Toland, J. (1814) *A New Edition of Toland's History of the Druids by P. Huddleston* 1123.g.29

Tyler, F.C. (1939) *The Geometrical Arrangement of Ancient Sites* London, Simpkin Marshall D-07702.aaa.55

Wood, J.E. (1978) *Sun, Moon and Standing Stones* OUP x421/10666

Proceedings of the Society of Antiquaries of Scotland Ac.2770/2a *Recumbent Stone Circles* 88 Derivation from Clava tradition, p197

Walker, I. C. (1962/3) pp88–89 96 *The Clava Cairns* (in Ireland and Scotland) pp95–100 96

Burl, H. A. W. (1969/70) pp56–81 102 *Recumbent Stone Circles of North east Scotland*

Coles, J. M.; Taylor, J. J. p97 102 *Excavation of a Midden . . . Culbin Sands, Morayshi*
Stone Circles in Aberdeenshire

Dalrymple, C. E. (1884) 18 *Notes on the Excavation of the Stone Circle at Crichie, Aberdeenshire* pp319–25

Peter, J. (1885) 19 *Stone Circles in Old Deer* pp370–377

Coles, F. R. (1899/1900) 34 p139

Coles, F. R. (1900/1) 35 pp187–248

Coles, F. R. (1901/2) 36 pp488–581

Coles, F. R. (1902/3) 37 pp82–142

Coles, F. R. (1903/4) 38 pp256–306

Coles, F. R. (1904/5) 39 pp190–206

Coles, F. R. (1905/6) 40 *Stone Circles* pp164–206

Coles, F. R. (1906/7) 41 *Stone Circles in Banffshire and Morayshire* pp130–172 48 p191

Ritchie, J. (1916/7) *Notes on some Stone Circles in Central Aberdeenshire* pp30–47

Ritchie, J. (1917/8) *Cup Marks on the Stone Circles and Standing Stones of Aberdeenshire and Part of Banffshire* pp86–121

Ritchie, J. (1918/9) *Notes on some Stone Circles in S Aberdeenshire and N Kincardineshire* pp64–79

Ritchie, J. (1919/20) 54 *The Stone Circle at Broomed of Critchie*

Ritchie, J. (1922/3) *Stone Circles at Raedykes nr Stonehaven* pp20–28

Ritchie, J. (1925/60) 60 *Folklore of the Aberdeenshire Stone Circles and Standing Stones* pp304–313

Keiller (1927) *Interim Report – Stone Circles of Aberdeenshire and Kingardnshire Scheduled as Ancient Monuments*

Kilbride-Jones, H. E. (1933/4) *Stone Circles: A New Theory of the Erection of the Monoliths* pp81–99

Kilbride-Jones, H. E. (1934/5) 69 *Excavations: Loanhead of Daviot and Cullerlie* pp169–204

Kilbride-Jones, H. E. (1935/6) 70 *A Late Bronze Age Cemetery – Loanhead of Daviot* pp278–310

Aberdeen, Third Spalding Club (1932) *The Third Spalding Club: What is it, etc* Ac.8246(6)

Aberdeen and North of Scotland Library and Information Co-operative Service (1982) *A Directory of Library Resources in the North East of Scotland* compiled by Susan Semple (2nd edition) x950/15761

The Kirkyard of . . .

Discovery and Excavation, Scotland

New Statistical Account of Scotland Vol xii Aberdeenshire (Edin 1843)

Old Statistical Account of Scotland

Ordnance Survey Name Books

10. Certain other 'French' ultra-left currents from this period are more accessible to the general reader because individuals involved with them later became famous academics. Both Cornelius Castoriadis and Jean-François Lyotard were active in the Socialism Or Barbarism group and collections of their political writings are available in reliable English translations published by reputable academic presses. S ou B emerged from the Chaulieu-Montal tendency within the Trotskyist Fourth International (French section). Their 1948 break with this organisation entailed both an uncompromising denunciation of Trotskyism and a total rejection of the absurd notion that

the USSR was a 'degenerate workers' state'. From the beginning S ou B contained two distinct currents represented by Chaulieu (the pseudonym of Castoriadis, who favoured a revolutionary party) and Montal (the pseudonym of Lefort, who was for the spontaneous self-organisation of workers). Unhappily, Lefort has to date failed to attract supporters within English-language academic publishing. Only by grasping the respective positions of both Castoriadis and Lefort is it possible understand how S ou B attracted elements from both the councilist and Bordigist poles of the French ultra-left.

11. No doubt the anachronistic quality of Grassic Gibbon's work, the stress on form and repetition, stems in part from the fact that he had to slip his writings out through a small hole in the side of the dressmaker's dummy in which he lived after his wife had imprisoned him there rather than admit to friends that her husband wasn't the pseudo-metaphysical poet and critic William Empson who'd been educated at Winchester and Magdalene College, Cambridge. That said, for Gibbon to act, to create, to satisfy desire was paramount, despite moral uncertainty and the difficulty of moving his arms around inside the dummy. Gibbon's work is terrible in all senses of the word but especially in the sense of wearing a brown felt dressing gown which was ragged at the edge over a pair of sequined orthopaedic panty hose in a whorehouse where the girls wouldn't even look at him unless they were doped. Indeed, about the only good thing you can say about Gibbon is that he avoided the academic training that causes the likes of Bo Fowler and Robert Irwin to appear so petulantly pedantic in their attempts to make Eng. Lit. look 'left-field' despite the tediously even tone of their prose and a desperate desire that this should be recognised as 'style' ha ha.

12. Alternatively I might have begun and thus ended, perhaps begun again would be a more accurate description, with an extended version of the following 'improvisation': A man no

longer called Alan came to Aberdeen. He told me his name was Callum. Somewhere along the line he slipped out of my life. The life slipped out of Callum. If I could reach out and touch him. Reach out. Touch him. Slipped. Slipped out. Life slipped out. Along the line. He slipped out. My life. If I could slip out. If I could reach out. A man. A man called Callum. No longer. He slipped out of my life. If I could slip out of my life. Reach out and touch. Reach out and touch him. Reach out and touch him somewhere along the line. He slipped out. He slipped out of Aberdeen. The life slipped out of him. A man called Alan came to Aberdeen. A man called Alan came to Aberdeen with me. Alan left Aberdeen. Alan slipped out of this life. Alan and Callum came to Aberdeen. A man called Callum changed his name to Alan and I am no longer sure whether or not I killed him.

He told me his name was Callum. Somewhere along the line he slipped out of my life. A man no longer called Alan came to Aberdeen. If I could reach out and touch him. The life slipped out of Callum. Touch him. Reach out. Slipped out. Slipped. Along the line. Life slipped out. My life. He slipped out. If I could reach out. If I could slip out. A man called Callum. A man. He slipped out of my life. No longer. Reach out and touch. If I could slip out of my life. Reach out and touch him somewhere along the line. Reach out and touch him. He slipped out of Aberdeen. He slipped out. A man called Alan came to Aberdeen. The life slipped out of him. Alan left Aberdeen. A man called Alan came to Aberdeen with me. Alan and Callum came to Aberdeen. Alan slipped out of this life. A man called Callum changed his name to Alan and I am no longer sure whether or not I killed him.

Alan and Callum came to Aberdeen. A man no longer called Alan came to Aberdeen. Alan left Aberdeen. He told me his name was Callum. A man called Alan came to Aberdeen with me. Somewhere along the line he slipped out of my life. The life slipped out of him. The life slipped out of Callum. He slipped out. If I could reach out and touch him. Reach out and touch him. If I could slip out of my life. No longer. Reach out. A man. Touch him. If I could reach out. Slipped. My life. Slipped out. He slipped out. Along the line. Life slipped out. If I could slip out. A man called Callum. He slipped out of my life. Reach out and touch. Reach out and touch him somewhere along the line. He slipped out of Aberdeen. A man called Alan came to Aberdeen. Alan slipped out of this life. A man called Callum changed his name to Alan and I am no longer sure whether or not I killed him.

A man no longer called Alan came to Aberdeen. Alan and Callum came to Aberdeen. He told me his name was Callum. Alan left Aberdeen. Somewhere along the line he slipped out of my life. A man called Alan came to Aberdeen with me. The life slipped out of Callum. The life slipped out of him. If I could reach out and touch him. He slipped out. If I could slip out of my life. Reach out and touch him. Reach out. No longer. A man. If I could reach out. Touch him. My life. Slipped. He slipped out. Slipped out. Life slipped out. Along the line. A man called Callum. If I could slip out. Reach out and touch. He slipped out of my life. He slipped out of Aberdeen. Reach out and touch him somewhere along the line. Alan slipped out of this life. A man called Alan came to Aberdeen. A man called Callum changed his name to Alan and I am no longer sure whether or not I killed him. &c. &c. &c.